The Cool Side Of The Pillow

Perry Gamsby

The Cool Side Of The Pillow

Dedicated to all the Pete's, Debbie's, Nikki's, Don's, Hamish's, Clara's, Alena's, Chris' and even Terri's and John's, but never the Tim's!

"Just keep in mind that a few months ago your wonderful new soul mate, love of your life, best-thing-that ever-happened-to-you-woman was some other poor sod's bitch wife from hell…" One of my mates.

"Why get married? Just find someone you hate and buy them a house!"

Published by StreetWise Publications,

22 Waikanda Cres, Whalan, NSW 2770

http://streetwisepublications.info

http://perrygamsby.net

Copyright Perry Gamsby 2006, 2010, 2012

Author- Gamsby, Perry 1961-

First Edition limited run March 2006

Reprinted 2008, 2010

This Revised Edition 2012

ISBN 978-0-9806346-2-4

All Rights Reserved

Cast of Main Characters

Pete Graham, the victim of his wife's lust and greed.

Terri Graham, the wife who knew what she wanted and how to get it.

John Taylor , the spineless cuckold with more money than moral fibre.

Debbie Taylor, the "past her use by" wife of John and fellow victim.

Nikki (Hamish & Clara) A modern career woman with poor taste in men.

Don, a no hoper who left Nikki, permanently.

Tim, the toy boy from hell.

Alena (Jacky & Kayleen) a modern single mum doing her best.

Chris, a decent bloke with problems of his own.

The Story is set in Sydney, New South Wales, Australia, present day.

Author's Foreword

I originally began writing 'The Cool Side Of The Pillow' sometime before the divorce from my first wife came through. It was begun as therapy and indeed, it was very therapeutic. It allowed me to take the factual events and characters and infuse an element of fiction that made things turn out more how I wanted them to have turned out. In a word, it helped me to regain control of a major event in my life that was, from the very beginning, totally out of my control.

You can't make someone fall in love with you, they either do or they don't and that is their choice. Similarly, you can't stop them from ceasing to be in love with you; again it is their choice. No matter how hard you try, no matter what you do or say, if they choose to fall out of love, then they will.

I can't speak for women when it is they who are left for another by their spouse, but I know from the dozens of divorced and separated men I have spoken with, that this loss of control is a very real thing and a major element in the matrix that is divorce. Men are used to being in charge, in control to at least some degree and able to influence people and events in some way. You can't do it when she decides she wants to leave and live with someone else. It is her decision and not one you can force her to change. Perhaps once upon a time in our society you could, but not today and that is how it should be. In fact, I would say a lot of domestic violence is the result of the man being unable to accept that in this society at least, he is no longer 'Lord and Master'.

It is infinitely worse when he sees his children being fathered by another man, more so if it is the cuckold that took his wife, his pride and his dignity from him. At least that is how many see this. I was fortunate there were no children in our marriage and the divorce was clean and for the most part I guess one could say it was amicable. It still took me several years to get to the point where I was ready once again to settle down with another woman.

These were years in which I was able to do whatever I wanted to do because I was a mature adult male with a decent income and enough confidence and capabilities to tackle any challenge. I bought a small yacht and learned to sail, scaring myself silly in seas taller than my mast. I travelled around the world, learned to scuba dive and scared myself sillier chasing sharks and other sea creatures with bite. I bought a Land Rover and explored the roughest terrain I could find, pitting myself and my machine against whatever Australia could throw at me.

Then one day, coming back from a scuba diving trip down south of Sydney our mini-bus was stuck in traffic. Everyone on the bus reached for their mobile phones to tell their loved ones they would be late home. Who was I going to call? My dog never answered the phone as his paws made it too difficult. I realised then I was ready to share my life once more and within a year I was married again, five years after I received my decree absolute. In those five years I had heard from my ex-wife just twice when she had rung me for whatever reason and both times I had said nothing, for I had nothing to say to her.

During those years I had ceased needing to write this book for therapy and had in fact put it aside. After I was once again in love and happily married, I took it out of the drawer, blew off the dust and made the decision it had to be finished. I did just that and then self-published just ten copies, all I could afford. The formatting was atrocious and the typos too numerous and when I read it over just recently, each and every one of the 65,000 or so words, I felt the story deserved to be presented in a better way. If I had learned anything over the years since self-publishing the first edition it was how to properly format a book.

I fixed the typos and I rewrote some of the sentences but overall I confess I left it pretty much as it was when it was finished, some six or seven years after the events fictionalized within. It was what I was feeling back then and short of tidying up some grammatical gaffs and overuse of semi colons I felt it should stand as it was.

This is a work of fiction, based on events that really happened and the actual people who were a part of those events. Some of these people are composites of more than one or two real people and some of the events happened to others than those portrayed in the story; but there is a lot of truth in these pages. There is also a lot of fiction, too, so don't try to figure out which is which, just read, and hopefully enjoy, the story.

Perry Gamsby, January 2012

CHAPTER 1

Don knew his time was drawing close. Suicides have that gift. Alone in all of God's creatures they have the ability to choose the time and manner of their demise. For some, it is a rational decision based more on logic than emotion. For others, perhaps the majority, it is a fairly spur of the moment act that has been a long time coming. Who in their right mind wakes up and thinks, "I'll end it all now, in the drawing room with the revolver."?

Don knew he was getting closer. All he needed was a trigger. Something he could use to justify ending it all. Then he'd show her, and them, all of them. A fight, an argument, behaviour out of character and socially reprehensible should do the trick. It had worked for him in the past when he needed to manipulate some situations. He had come close before. Even to the point of standing on the cliff edge. The Police Rescue Squad had turned up, right after the ambulance and her. Don was glad she was there to witness what she had caused. Of course the counselor had 'convinced' him it was not her fault. Don had made the right mouth noises and been allowed to get on with his life. Easy.

This time he was going through with it. He would teach her a lesson she'd never forget. It never occurred to him he wouldn't be around to witness her grief and distress. If it had, he would have thought the whole thing through and realised it was not the best plan after all. But if he could think like that, he would not be contemplating suicide in the first place, would he?

*****

Nikki had had enough. It was the mental abuse that really got to her. Constantly being told you are ugly, unwanted and unloved took effect sooner or later. Her self-esteem was dragging along behind her like a wedding train, ripped apart and trodden on by all and sundry. Now he had struck her. Hard. Across the face. The sting of the blow still echoed tactilely across her bruised nerve endings. The pain was made worse by the fact her two children had stood there and recorded it all for their posterity. So had his two kids. All four of them were crying. Trust him to leave her to clean up his emotional mess once again. This has got to stop. She was leaving him. This time she meant it.

*****

Terri cried silently, the sobs of despair racking her lithe body and making her beautiful face ugly with the intensity of her feelings. She hadn't meant to go this far. It had all gotten out of control. Or had it? She knew all along what she was doing, what she was risking. But the risk had seemed worth it at the time. And only time would tell how it would all end. And what was the end? How would she know when she had reached the end? Would she start again, reborn and happy? Or would her life continue on in a never ending cycle of shame and hopelessness? She loved her husband, truly loved him. But what he could give her was not enough. Not enough money, not enough security, not enough life, not enough future. He was a good man and gave all he had, but that was not enough. She wanted more out of life. She deserved more than what he could ever give. He would be devastated she knew, but she had to be strong and see this through to the end. Whatever the end might be. She only hoped she would know it when she got there.

*****

Pete was blissfully ignorant of the impending doom that was about to visit his life and change everything forever. He was blissfully happy, too. He'd just managed a terrific career change at the age of 35 and was starting out on a new job in a new industry and he was very happy. He dreamt of how much his life, Terri's too, would change now he had the chance to do what he loved for his living. Do what you love and do it massively and you will never work a day in your life and you'll be truly successful. That's what his latest self help book was preaching. Pete believed it because it made sense. He had so many plans for him and Terri. Their life together would go from strength to strength and he was the happiest man in the world.

*****

Don still had half a glass of red in his hand when the carbon monoxide took its toll. He had been drifting off to sleep, his mind full of confused thoughts of anger and revenge when death took him gently in her arms and carried him away. The car radio played on, adding a sound track to his lonely death that no scriptwriter would ever dream of trying out on an audience. The car vibrated to the purr of the motor as he disappeared from this world in all but body. His mind ceased its tortured wanderings and his soul prepared itself for an eternity in damnation.

*****

Nikki parked at the head of the driveway and looked down at Don's car. Music escaped from the closed vehicle as she took a few tentative steps towards the Ford. She could see Don sitting in the passenger seat, slightly slumped against the window and looking away from her. She steeled herself to open the door and tell him she was leaving him. She had only tracked him down so she could make arrangements for the children. His, not hers. She loved them almost as her own, but they were his responsibility and she had enough on her plate right now as it was.

She pulled on the driver's side door handle but the door was locked. Walking around the front of the car meant she missed seeing the hose from the exhaust running up and into the back window. She wasn't taking in details anyway. She was too hyped up for that. Her focus was on Don and what his reaction would be and could she get away in time if he took another swing at her.

Nikki didn't need to open the door to see Don was dead. Even if it was unlocked she had no need to open the door, reach in and feel for a pulse. His eyes were still closed but she knew instinctively he wasn't asleep. Shaking her head, she stepped back and then for the first time she took in the hose and the newspaper stuffed into the back window. The pain shot through her arm as she smashed her hand, palm first into the window and screamed. All of the abuse and anger of the last twelve months came out in a choked, agonising moan of anguish and hatred. A keening howl that would chill the blood and make any man's hair stand on end. Hatred that he had run away like the coward he'd always been, deep down inside. "You bastard." she thought. "You lousy, stinking, cowardly bastard.."

At the time Nikki found Don, Terri was finding her knickers, kicked off under the hotel bed in a fit of lust and desire that was not totally directed at John. But she didn't know that because she was not tuned in to her sub-conscious mind at that time, only the tiny part of the brain that stimulates sexual arousal. This was different to the first time. The first time he had paid for her services like all the others. Then spent the remaining fifty five minutes of his hour crying on her shoulder about how his wife didn't understand him and how he was rolling in money but had no one he lusted enough for to share it with. That's not exactly how he described it but then he wasn't listening to his sub-conscious at the time, either. He'd just met a beautiful creature who didn't really belong in this B-Grade brothel. A classic case of what's a nice whore like you doing in a place like this?

"I have to go to Singapore on business, Terri. Just for three days next month. I want you to come with me."

Terri was thrilled, yet frightened at the same time. She loved to travel but how would she explain to Pete where she would be for that time? A precious few days that would be worth a month here at home. She knew she would go, after all this was why John had seemed so attractive in the first place. As a top executive in charge of the country's biggest chain of shopping malls, he was on over three hundred grand a year. He had made sure she knew it, too. The jewellery, the expensive restaurants, this top hotel. "Sure. I'll have to come up with something to tell Pete, but I want to go. I hear the shopping is terrific." Already she was feeling the agony and the ecstasy of the double life she had been leading for months now. She would fool Pete easy enough. She felt guilty but she had her dream, her plan and she was going to see it through. Besides, she was starting to feel something for John. Maybe it was because he was the only person who knew her secret, the only one she could unburden herself to.

"That's great. You'll have to sit in economy, it would look too suss if you sat up in business with me. Besides, my secretary and my wife are good friends. I don't want Debbie knowing until I'm ready to leave her."

Terri's last thoughts as she pulled on her lacy G-string was to remember a few lines she had once heard. Something about, "Oh what a tangled web we weave, when we begin, to deceive..." or words to that effect. She knew now exactly what the saying meant.

Pete lay back, one arm cradling his head. Beside him Terri was asleep again, just as she had been when he made love to her. It had been like it was in the beginning. The frenzy of the initial coupling as two strangers learn each other's inner secrets for the first time, never to be the same again, almost like losing your virginity.

He had been half way into a deep sleep when Terri turned to him and kissed him. Hard. They hadn't been intimate for several months now, since shortly after she went back to working in the restaurant. He didn't mind her working as a lingerie waitress again. They needed the money and she was bored with the two bit factory job she had held for two years after they moved out of the city. It meant she worked nights and stayed with a girlfriend as it was too late to drive all the way home by the time the place closed at two or three am. He'd offered to come and pick her up but she had almost screamed him down, saying he needed his sleep to be fresh at work the next day. She was right, but... Anyway, she was home tonight and all of a sudden kissing him with a passion he had missed over the years of their marriage as lust gave way to love and familiarity, then to a comfortable feeling of security and then to once a week if they were lucky. But she had been frozen and aloof for weeks now. At first he thought it was his snoring and he tried every cure he could to give her a good night's rest. Then the complaint was he was lazy and did nothing around the house. Now he raced home and made the place tidy for her, washing the dishes and vacuuming the carpets. But still she alienated him. And now she was in his arms once again.

"You taste of lollies" she said dreamily between kisses. Pete didn't follow what she meant, even though she said it three or four times. He felt between her legs and was surprised at how hot and wet she had become already. He was ready too, and not about to miss a chance like this. He climbed astride her and began to revel once again in her recalcitrant refuge. He was almost there when she started screaming, beating him with her fists. He rolled away in utter shock and surprise, lying propped on one arm as he looked at his demented wife.

"Who are you?" Terri asked, "Who are you? You're raping me!" Terri was obviously in shock and Pete knew she honestly believed she had been raped. What had happened between the explosion of passion and the chill of awakening?

"I've never raped anyone in my life, Terri. I'm not about to start with my own wife. I don't know who you were screwing, but I know it wasn't me." Pete rolled on to his side so his back was to her. He almost sobbed with desperation. He was firmly convinced Terri was suffering from

Depression. Now it seemed she was becoming delusional. He rolled onto his back and lay there, listening to her soft breathing. Almost as quickly as she had begun raving she had calmed down and was now soundly asleep. Pete loved his wife and vowed he would stick with her through this. He would stay until she was better, he would never desert her. He had always believed the brain was like any other organ or part of the body. It could get sick just like a heart or a liver. But instead of trouble climbing stairs or urinating in technicolour, you behaved differently from normal and your thought processors were messed up. If only he could get her to see a doctor, maybe there was medication that would help.

*****

Debbie was suspicious. She had John's credit card account laid out on the table in front of her. She cross referenced the dates on the account with her own diary, his days interstate and overseas, highlighted. Blind Freddy could put two and two together without any help. John was having an affair. How else could you stay in the best hotel in this town at the same time as you are supposedly in Melbourne? She even had his mobile phone account placed alongside so she could confirm his calls to her on those particular nights were made from Sydney. He rang her three, sometimes four times a day. Always had. She knew something was up because he was so much perkier these last few weeks. The sex had been better than ever, too.

The entry for the sixth of March stood out. One hundred and eighty six dollars spent at Crest pty ltd, Hornsby, for 'services'? That was the night he had come home late, almost jumping out of his skin. "Oh Dee, I'm so horny" he had begged her as he climbed into bed. Debbie had done her wifely duty, surprised at the vigor with which he took her. He hadn't been like this since she first took his cherry. He'd been nineteen and working his way through college at the bar she managed. She was thirty three, still sexy and going through a messy divorce. Now she was forty eight and showing her age. He was thirty four and, she was sure, tired of her.

He still loved her, no doubt about that, needed her even. In the way psychologists would have described a classic Oedipus complex. But someone else was lighting his fire. Some young floozy. Debbie didn't pick up on the generation gap giveaway a term like floozy connotated. She just let the tears roll down her cheeks and soak the bills lying in front of her on the big kitchen table they had bought together when they moved back to Sydney.

Debbie looked again at the irrefutable evidence in front of her. Proof her man was up to no good. Well she was going to find out who this slut was and she would fight for her man. And her baby. She already had two grown up daughters from her first marriage and she knew this would be her last chance to have a child. John's child. She looked back at her diary, the sixth marked in red because that was when her temperature had been at its highest. That night of mad love making had succeeded in giving her what she had always wanted. But now the child would become a weapon in her fight for her man. She would use everything in her arsenal, including the fetus growing in her womb if necessary. Everything.

*****

Nikki was staring at the empty glass. She'd finished staring at the empty bottle whilst the glass was still half full. Or was that only half empty? Her mind refused to struggle with the complexities of that half remembered message on a coffee cup. Or was it one of those cheap posters you used to buy and hang in the toilet? Her mind skipped a track and flipped back to the funeral. Almost like the whole event was stage managed by a funeral director recently kicked out of producers school for being too cliché, it had even begun to rain as they stood around the grave. Don had thought of everything, even taking out funeral insurance and pre-paying for a plot in an expensive lawn cemetery.

She had cried during the service, at the grave and again back at Don's parent's house. People she didn't know from a bar of soap had offered their condolences. What exactly was a condolence, anyway? Could you pick one up at the grocery store? "I'll have a loaf of bread, a litre of milk and do you have any of those condolences, yeah ...the big ones for truly great losses?" Her mind flipped back again to the glass. She had another bottle of scotch somewhere. But one was enough. She wasn't going to go over the edge. She had her children to think off. Don's kids had been whisked away by their mother and her parents within hours of being informed of Don's death. They hadn't said it so much as projected the message that Don would still be here if he had still been with Carey. But Carey, the first wife and archetypal shrew was what had kicked Don off in the first place. Her affair with his best mate. Her affair with their neighbour. And his wife. And all through it ripping him apart with her vitriol and caustic spittle. When Nikki met Don he was so far out on the limb he couldn't climb back in. She'd had to build a tree house around him, a tree house of love and trust. A tree house that, like all tree houses, eventually blew down in one of life's frequent storms.

Oh God! She was sick of thinking in metaphors and similes. The reality of the situation was that he was dead and she was left to carry on. He escaped the day to day drain of filling in time from the cradle to the grave whilst she was left to clean up the mess and get on with it. He was free to continue on the great journey and she had to pay off his ticket. Christ she had bills coming out of her kazoo. Mortgage, car payments, credit cards, school fees, rates, you name it, she knew all of them by the feel of the thick bundle of mail she pulled daily from the mail box. Bills, even wrapped in a thick rubber band and bundled together to protect the innocent articles of mail had a feel all their own.

The unsolicited advertising, or junk mail as those not in marketing called them, were a nuisance, but sometimes of passing interest. The letters starting, "Dear Nikki, I just heard and I'm so...." So what? Sad? Sorry? Sickened? Try pissed off! Because that was the best way Nikki could describe how she felt about it. Pissed off! Four years of university, two years post graduate study, not to mention twelve years of private school education and the most apt description she could think of was.. "Pissed Off!" Should be all capitals, 'PISSED OFF!'

So what? What next? Bed. A good cry to rock her to sleep then up to face another day. Brave face for the kids and those few die hard well-wishers still tapping softly on her door and then, back to the kitchen table. They had agonized for weeks over that table. He had wanted a glass topped pseudo modern monstrosity. She won out with the solid timber colonial in pine with a jarrah stain to match the sideboard. They'd paid an extra hundred for the stain and another hundred to have it stressed. Stressed. What a joke. A hundred bucks to have some cabinet maker beat the crap out of it with a hammer. Don should have saved the money and used her head. That's how the side board got the dent in the left door. It would have been a matching set. And what a conversation piece. She could set up her own business designing furniture inspired by random acts of domestic violence. She'd make a.....a ...a killing. The tears started again, only this time they were accompanied on their slow slick trail south by a moan that came from the depths of her soul. Damn you Don!

CHAPTER 2

"It's fifty dollars an hour, fifty cents per kilometre plus disbursements."

"What are disbursements?" Debbie asked.

"Expenses, title searches, fees. You'll get receipts, plus a full report, photo's, everything."

The private investigator was not what Debbie had imagined. Probably seen too many TV shows. This guy was youngish, intelligent and appeared genuine. Trustworthy. He had put her at ease on the phone when he tried to talk her out of spending her money tailing her husband.

"Surveillance is a long, costly and rarely satisfying method of obtaining the proof you want, Debbie." Jack Regan went on. "I could sit outside his home or office for hours and lose him within the first hundred metres. Sydney traffic is not like on TV. You never get a parking spot right across from the entrance, you can't sit more than one car back without losing him at the first traffic light and he'll spot a single tail within minutes if he's switched on. The police use several vehicles, some in front, some behind and some running parallel streets when they do surveillance. And still they lose their mark. They have radios, tracking devices and anything else they need. You can't afford more than one guy for a few hours. Say hubby goes into a block of flats. So what? Half the flats will have women in them, maybe more. How do you prove he saw anyone, let alone did anything? Save your money."

Then she told him about the credit card bills, mobile phone account, all the information she had gathered together.

"O.K. Now you have something. I'll pop by about two and have a chat. If I think I can help, I'll need the first five hundred up front. Let's work that off and see what we get before you spend any more."

And now he was here. In their kitchen. At their kitchen table. Telling her exactly how he would go about ripping their marriage apart for her, because that is exactly what would happen if he did his job right. Providing she wasn't mistaken and he didn't think she was. His first question had been to ask what she hoped to achieve, what was her objective. To prove John was being unfaithful she said. Then what? She didn't know. But she knew she had to be sure in her own mind what she was certain of in her heart.

"Right. I'll do a company search on this Crest Pty Ltd. My guess it is the registered business name of a brothel. They'll be trading under some alluring title but have the credit card merchant's account set up with something like this to avoid embarrassment. The top places use a restaurant as a cover. Easier to explain away a business dinner than just 'services'. If we get lucky there, I'll check the place out to confirm it's what we think. Then we might look at doing some surveillance on that place. At least place him at the scene. A bit hard to bluff your way out of that. I'll also check out these numbers on his phone bill. Make a pretence call and see what we come up with. I'm hoping he is calling her. If I get a female I'll run a check with a contact I have and see if we can get a name and address from the phone number. That will cost $250, he's risking his job, so it's money well spent. Once we get that we can build a dossier on her and then review your choices. O.K?"

Debbie nodded. She couldn't speak. Fear, or was it something else, gripped her stomach in a claw like hand and the sweet taste of adrenalin filled her mouth. She was excited, but scared. If she had ever been in combat she would have recognized the high straight away. A mixture of fear and excitement, the anticipation of great danger, the almost sexual relief of surviving. She felt it all.

*****

Pete was working the heavy bag, his wrapped and gloved fists beating a rapid tattoo on the leather sack stuffed with rags and his black belt. He didn't wear the thing anymore. He was past that. He used to run a big school, made a good living doing what he loved. But then Terri wanted a break to have kids and they couldn't get by with just his income from the school. It wasn't good enough for the two of them to live on the way Terri liked to live. So he went back to working a regular job. He hated it. He still taught a few loyal students a few nights a week, but it wasn't the same.

The three minute round came to an end in the clock in his head and he stretched out during his minute of rest. A quick look at the clock on the wall to confirm his own timing and he was into another round on the speed ball. He could time himself to within five or ten seconds. It was just practise, familiarity. Like anything it was hard at first but repetition worked its magic and now he could time his rounds without the clock. A bit like riding a bike, driving a car or even how we all learnt to walk. If we'd given up after the first tumble we'd all still be crawling.

He was working fast jab combinations. He'd done hooks the previous round. He was rusty and he felt it. It had been months since his last workout. He almost felt like confessing to the bag, "bag forgive me, it has been two months since my last workout." "Do ten rounds and light a candle for forgiveness, my son," the bag replied. Pete shook his head and put his mind back on the job in hand. He knew few successful boxers had any great amount of imagination. If they did they would imagine the pain of losing and not get in the ring. Only a handful of good boxers in history had been champions and able to pass the test for MENSA. Not that boxers had to be dumb to win, far from it. It was a thinking man's game, boxing. You needed brains as well as skill. And fitness. Lots of fitness. Pete didn't have the fitness, but he'd get it back. As for having too much imagination to be a great boxer, he didn't care. He was too old for a career anyway. Besides, he knew that with a lack of imagination came the blissful ability to become single minded and work only for the goal of becoming a champion. Too smart and you got bored before you got there. Pete knew himself well enough to know that he would never have stuck it out. All those hours in the gym, or running roadwork at six a.m. No, he'd be a gentleman boxer and do it for the fun and fitness. Now that Terri was working so much and away so often he had plenty of spare time to get back into it. He would rather see more of his wife but he suppressed his guilt at enjoying the personal time. He even suppressed those random thoughts that came into his head from time to time. Like what if Terri left him, would that be so bad? He'd have time to do whatever he wanted. No! Perish the thought. But he had thought it. What was that about your sub-conscious knowing all, if only you would be smart enough to tune in and take heed?

*****

Terri was lying back in his arms. She was starting to really fall for John. He was different to Pete, more vulnerable. He really needed her and he could provide her with much more security than Pete. At first she had only intended to work in the brothel as a receptionist. But then she saw the money those fat slags were making. She was much prettier than any of them. They knew it and they were jealous. A couple of them had tried to give her a hard time her first night as a worker. But Terri, as fragile as she appeared and as warm as a friendly puppy, was made of sterner stuff. She had her plan and nothing was getting in her way. Nothing and no-one. John had been one of her first. As he talked to her about his old hag of a wife and their palatial home in Queensland, the big executive residence in Castle Hill and the stocks and bonds, she realised this was the sort of security Pete should be providing for her. The plan had started to form in her mind almost of its own accord, as if it had been there all along. She would let the client fall in love with her. She would milk him for all he was worth and her and Pete could live happily ever after on the proceeds. One big sting and she could be free of this job, this double life and never have to worry again.

As they say, the best laid plans.... By now Terri had switched her allegiance from the man she had loved, vowed to love forever, to the new opportunity. She no longer thought of how she could wrest his wealth from him and share it with Pete. Now she thought of how she could free her lover from the clutches of the old hag. It was a kind of Stockholm Syndrome in a domestic setting. Of course Terri didn't know about the Stockholm Syndrome, she had never been a hostage or a bank robber. Or trained to assault buildings. Pete had, the assault part, not the robbery bit. He knew all about the Syndrome. He just didn't know about John. But that, as is the case in all things, would soon change.

*****

Jack was having a good day, the kind of day when things just kept falling into place. Crest Pty Ltd was a brothel, owned by Dallah Pty Ltd, another computer generated shelf company name. If he tracked back far enough he'd find who were the directors and shareholders of the parent company, but that wasn't his objective. He'd talked to the real estate agents who managed the property and they had confirmed the brothel known as 'Heaven's Gate' at the given address was run by Crest. Point one. Now to check out hubby's mobile phone calls.

He started with the number that appeared most often on the bill. Debbie had identified three of the seven different numbers, one was hers, one their best friend and the other her girlfriend. She had been staying with Carol, the girlfriend, one night whilst he was away and he had called her there. It checked with one of the nights in a Sydney hotel when he should have been in Perth, so maybe he was making sure she was tucked up safe and sound?

The other four had all been called once, except for one which had fifteen calls listed against it. Regular. A pattern. Jack liked patterns. People were creatures of habit, that's how they got caught.

*****

A young woman's voice answered his call. "Hi." Soft, questioning, giving nothing away.

"Hello, this is Jack from Vodaphone Customer Service." The first four digits had told him which phone company she was with. "We have received your complaint and I am just touching base to let you know it is being investigated and that we will not be taking any action to recover the outstanding amount whilst we look into this."

"What complaint? I haven't..."

Jack broke in, keeping up the pressure and making sure she was off guard so he could slip in the sixty four thousand dollar question and not make it too obvious. "We are pretty sure our equipment is correct, but occasionally we do make a glitch." You couldn't just ring up and ask for a name and address and not expect her to be suspicious.

"But I haven't..." She insisted.

"Our records show those calls were made from your phone, and we don't have any proof of payment. '

"Look, I haven't..."

"Haven't what?" Jack probed.

"Haven't made a complaint and my account is paid up."

"Well your number is oh four nine seven, five five three two one one, isn't it?

"Yes", she replied.

Jack tensed then forced himself to relax, the next question had to sound natural, in order and not suspicious. "And your name is...?" He let it hang in the air.

"Terri Graham"

"Yes, and your billing address?" Go for the throat.

""22 Leyland Place, Whalan" She rattled it off with the unthinking familiarity we all have for something we know off by heart.

YES! Jack tried to keep the excitement out of his voice as he wound the call up. "Whalan Tasmania?" Slight rising inflection on the last syllable.

"No, Sydney."

"I'm sorry, we have a Miss T., no first name, Graham listed here. From a different address in Tassie. I think we might have taken down the number wrong, maybe one of the digits should be a four but looks like a nine or something like that." He let her finish off, knowing she would be eager to clear up the confusion and not have to pay someone else's bill.

"Yeah, that happens. But I am not that person and my account is paid up." Terri spoke with the authority of a once confused person suddenly being relieved to find they were not at fault after all. "You should check your records, what if you billed me for calls I didn't make?"

"That's impossible, each Sim card has its own Imei number, different to the phone number." Jack had had his own share of problems with the phone company and knew a little of the jargon. Enough to sound convincing. "Look, Miss Graham..."

"Mrs" Terri corrected him.

"Sorry, Mrs Graham. I'm sorry for the inconvenience. Please accept my apologies and please forget this call ever happened. I've had a rough couple of days with my youngest in the hospital and I don't want to lose my job for making a few mistakes." Hit the woman with the sympathy angle and she was sure to get all clucky.

"Oh, it was no bother. I hope your baby gets better." Terri was genuine in her concern for the voice on the other end of the phone. But Jack had known she would be and he needed that to pull out of the call safely. Women were so predictable in these areas. Mind you, it had cost him two wives by the time he was thirty three to learn that.

"Thank you, Mrs Graham, sorry to bother you, good day." She mumbled her goodbyes as he quickly cut the connection. So now he had a name, an address and the fact she was married. Now it was worth putting in surveillance. Not on hubby, but her. If she worked at the 'Heaven's Gate', BINGO! It was rarely this easy, but sometimes you got lucky. Pity, she sounded like a real sweet thing. If she was a looker he might use her services and bill the client. Purely for the reasons of providing irrefutable evidence, of course. The hooker was a looker. He chuckled at his simple wit as he started to plan the surveillance. Step one, get out the street directory and locate 22 Leyland Place, Whalan. Whalan? Wasn't that one of those housing commission estates now up for first home buyers? Miles out west and full of social security bludgers. Anyway, he had a terrific result, now to get to work.

*****

A day or two later, Terri had forgotten about the phone call when she picked up her mobile phone and her car keys and headed for the car. She didn't have to go to work this early but it meant she avoided having to talk to Pete. She felt guilty, ashamed and grubby. But she was starting to build her mental shield by convincing herself Pete was to blame. It was easier than accepting responsibility for her own actions.

Forty minutes later she pulled into the car park at the rear of the parlour, none of the girls called it a brothel, and found a space for the old BMW. Grabbing her bag she locked the car and headed for the staff entrance at the rear. She rang the buzzer and was rewarded with the hum of the electric lock releasing the catch. Pushing open the discreetly armoured door she went inside and headed for the girl's change room.

*****

Yes, she is a looker, Jack thought. He'd picked her up from Whalan after a quick drive by told him the car she would be driving. A 1983 BMW 735i. A nice limo like car in its day, now worth maybe ten grand or so. Still, a nice ride for a nice ride. He laughed silently at his pun and got the Nikon into operation. After she had headed towards the brothel he had sped past her and got here with a few minutes to spare. He'd checked out likely observation points on his previous visit, even identified the staff carpark and entrance. Time spent in reconnaissance, as his old sergeant used to say, is never wasted. He'd taken a risk not following her all the way here. What if she had been going shopping? Or off to meet hubby somewhere else but nearby? Well, risk was what made the job interesting.

He loved the sound of the motor drive reeling off multiple shots. Just like in the movies. This would give him a reason to hit the client for more dough. Sure, he was coming up with the goods, but then that's when you milked them for all you could. He was sick of worker's comp jobs and taking statements from stolen vehicle claimants for insurance companies. It was good bread and butter stuff, but tended to be a little boring. A nice little domestic job where you could get a good result was manna from heaven. Too many of these kind of jobs were the product of wifely paranoia with no chance of proving what didn't exist. Try telling that to the injured party after she got your bill for x number of hours.

Yes, she was a looker. Time to let her get settled, then go in and have some fun. All in the interests of doing a thorough job, of course. Got to give the client value for money, after all.

*****

Nikki put the box down and looked around at the mess moving house always seemed to create. She knew from experience it would take several days, even weeks, to unpack everything and tidy the place up. It would have been easier with Don to help, but he wouldn't be helping anyone now. Thinking about him made her sit down and start crying again. This was becoming a regular occurrence. Of course it didn't help to be moving into the house they had bought together, settlement coming only a week before he died. Died? He killed himself. Suicide. The word stuck in her mental craw as she wondered why the newspapers didn't publish reports on the nation's number one cause of death. Too depressing and something the pollies couldn't throw money at and fix. Suicides only made the papers if the coward took out the rest of the family as he went. Murder-suicide was printable. Plain old knock yourself off wasn't. Consequently, the people left behind had little in the way of support services or tax payer funded grief counseling. Simply left to get on with it and yet they were the true victims.

She looked again at the pile of boxes, crates and haphazardly strewn plastic bags of clothes filling the room. Her two children were outside, exploring the garden with the puppy they had bought only last month. A new start, new home, new pet, new life. Nikki stopped crying as suddenly as she had begun, another symptom her doctor had said would happen and quite normal, to be expected etc. Well, she would cry herself a river, as the old song said. Then she would get on with her life and eschew men for ever. Weak men who hit women especially. Except they all seemed so nice and desirable when you first met them. Then the first hit would make you wonder what you had done to cause it. You would convince yourself you were at fault and try harder to please. He would take everything you would give as his due and toss you an emotional table scrap from time to time so you would continue to chase after him. The next time he hit you would make you berate yourself for making him unhappy again. It took quite a few hits before you would realise he was the one in the wrong. But by then, it was too late. She worried if she was the type of woman who had a thing for violent men, wife bashers. If she was genetically doomed to one smack artist after another. It was too hard to contemplate so she took refuge in the emptying of the closest box. Kitchenware, and she was in a bedroom. Typical.

CHAPTER 3

Debbie was in shock. She sat silent and still whilst Jack Regan, Private Investigator, tore her world into little pieces. The evidence was irrefutable, but she had known the truth all along. It was just so much more painful now there was no doubt left to blindly cling to.

"And this photo shows Mrs Graham entering 'Heaven's Gate'" Jack was speaking in his best 'just the facts, ma'am' voice. He found it helped to keep the emotional forces under check. Right now his client would be stunned and responding mostly on auto-pilot. He laid the last photo on the table and looked at his client, her head on her chest, eyes staring at the floor.

Debbie looked up and saw the compassion in Jack's eyes. He had tried to warn her, after all. But she had to be sure. Now she was sure she wished she wasn't. Oh God! "She is beautiful, isn't she? So young, and married?"

"Yes, to a Peter Graham. They still co-habit at the house in the first photo. Nice little place, well kept garden, coupla dogs and cats. I don't think he knows what she does for a living, definitely he would be unaware of his wife's involvement with John."

"How do you know that?" asked Debbie.

"John's still alive. This guy, have a look at this shot I took of him the next day, is rather large. On top of that he runs a self defence school that is touted in the martial arts magazines as being a reality based street fighting school. I made a pretense call to enquire about classes. He was a world champion martial artist, boxer of some note when he was younger and an ex-Army Special Forces advisor on explosives and booby traps. This is one guy you don't want to have coming after you. He also used to run his own private investigation firm a few years back. In other words, I'd say he is smart and lethal. Typically though, he seems a nice guy over the phone, very professional. I'd say if he was a thug you would have little to worry about. But this guy would get subtle, very subtle." Jack refrained from adding that he had asked a few colleagues who had been in the industry back when Pete was a P.I. and one of them knew him. His contact had confirmed Jack's estimation of the man and finished with a warning to make sure Jack was on the right side of the guy. Jack took the hint. In his game, full of macho wanna-be's and ex-everythings, when you came across a player with real potential, you kept well clear of them. It wasn't cowardice. It was a mutual respect, like two old lions that had been in enough scraps to know when it would cost one or both of them their lives if they fought. Not worth the risk.

"Do you think he would hurt John if he found out?"

"Do you want him to hurt John?" Jack threw back. Always answer a question with a question and see where it went.

"In a way, yes. But I want my husband back. A black eye might teach him a lesson, though."

"Debbie, this kind of guy doesn't mess about with black eyes. If he decides to poke his head up he'll go for the throat. He knows he would be suspect number one, so he would make it worth his while. You might as well get hung for a sheep as a lamb. No. If he does go ballistic, he'll make sure nobody can prove it was him. He'll have alibi's set in stone." At least that's how Jack would do it and he reckoned Pete was just as good as him, maybe better, maybe just a little out of practise. It wouldn't take him long to get back into shape, though. Those guys were like time bombs, some of them.

*****

The scotch bottle sang its siren song and smiled as Nikki walked over to the shelf she called her bar. The trance continued as she found a glass and unscrewed the cap. The scotch chuckled as it dived from the confines of the bottle into the freedom of the cut-glass swimming pool, only one short stroke away from free-styling down her throat. Once in her stomach it would send some of its forces straight into her bloodstream to lull her brain into believing this was good for her. Other units would work their way to her liver and kidneys, leaving behind time bombs set with delayed action fuses, waiting until sufficient explosive force had been built up before starting its destructive work on her internal organs. Blast damage would appear on her nose and face, tell tale signs she would ignore as she swallowed another contingent of colon culling commando's.

The scotch needed time to complete its campaign against her health and well-being. But this one, it knew, was there for the taking. This one would wage war against herself with battalions of booze and regiments of reckless remonstrations against the unchangeable fate Don had bequeathed her. It was simple mathematics. Nikki was past counting or caring as she poured another shot, slopped in a lessening amount of coke and poured down another dose of highland pain killer. Why the hell not, she thought. The kids were with their dad and she was left with a house full of broken promises and half lived dreams. Unpacked boxes, unstacked books, shelves yawning their need for literature to clothe their naked emptiness. Christ she got poetic when she was pissed. Pissed? She was past pissed and she knew it. Knew it in one of those rare moments of lucidity that kept fighting themselves to the surface of her self consciousness, despite the best efforts of her good friend mister scotch and coke. Forget the coke. Let's have the next one straight up.

*****

Terri walked out of the office, her pay in her hand. She was calm, in control and feeling the happiest she had since she started there three months ago. No more whoring for her. At least not professionally. She was going to leave Pete, move in with John and start her life again. No one had to know how she and John had met. She'd tell them they met at the Hilton, in the Marble Bar. As time went on, their circle of friends would change and even the old ones would forget the drama that the break-up would cause. After all, it wasn't their lives and most people were so self centered they only remembered what had happened to them. Besides, none of them would be so uncouth as to mention anything embarrassing in public and she had no control over what they said and thought in private. John was superior to most of them and his boss would never know the details. The phrase, 'sordid details' flashed into her mind. Her self defence mechanisms just as quickly flushed it out.

When she got to the new flat she would call Pete and tell him it was over, she wasn't coming back. No. He'd hunt her down and try to get her back. She knew he loved her desperately and he was very capable of finding the proverbial needle in a haystack. That's why she couldn't tell him there was someone else. He'd kill John. John had money and power but Terri knew he couldn't fight his way out of a wet paper bag.

She'd seen Pete put two muggers in hospital one night when they were living in the city and coming home from a movie. He'd pushed her behind him like she was a rag doll and put both muggers on the ground in two seconds flat. Then one had pulled a knife from his jacket and tried to slash at Pete's legs. The mugger had raised himself on one knee and was slashing like a threshing machine on overdrive. Pete kicked him in the head, then stomped on his face, using the kerb as an anvil. Then he had calmly taken her arm and walked her away, leaving the two criminals where they lay. Ten more yards and they were inside their little terrace house and Terri ran to the bathroom to vomit. That's why she didn't realise Pete had phoned for an ambulance for the muggers. She stayed hunched over the bowl on all fours for some time before crawling into bed, relieved at surviving the attack and shocked at how easily her husband had beaten those two men. That's why she didn't know he had gone back with the first aid kit and stayed with the muggers until the ambulance came. The streets of the inner city always reverberated to the scream and wail of sirens so she took no notice of one more winding down close to her house. She drifted off to sleep thinking her husband possessed a callous, mean streak that could produce violent behaviour of a kind she'd never before had to witness.

The truth was far different. Pete had reacted instinctively and fast. Just as he had been trained to react. The same way he trained his students. He had no choice. Give them an inch and they would cut up a mile of your intestines without blinking an eye. But Pete could never pick a fight or mug anyone. Or hit them cold bloodedly. It was his training that kept him cool under fire. Then, once the threat was neutralized, the heart pounded again and the legs went weak. But you hid the signs of fear and got on with the job. Once they were no longer a threat, then you could offer them first aid. Pete could not leave them lying in the gutter, but then he had no choice but to finish the knife wielder off. It had been him or them. Simple. His first responsibility was to get Terri safely inside and out of harms way. They might have had back-up waiting in the shadows. Stomping the guys head had been a vicious move, but Pete hadn't picked the fight. You try to take someone's life with a knife, you can't say 'time out.' when it starts to go wrong. That punk would have cut his throat and raped Terri given half a chance. So Pete wasn't ashamed of his actions, but he still felt sorry for an injured member of the human race. Regardless of why he was injured or who had injured him.

Terri only had her own recollections of that night to fill her thoughts as she drove to the new flat. She was scared. Her stomach was knotted and she felt like she would throw up any second. She fought to keep herself under control as she tried to remember the way to their 'love nest' as the tabloids would describe it. Pete had never raised his voice to her, let alone his hand. But then she had never done this to him, either. The shame and sense of betrayal enveloped her like a shroud.

*****

28

John wrapped Debbie in his arms and hugged her tightly. He was so full of happiness he was ready to burst. He had to tell Debbie about Terri. About how happy he was with her. How she made him feel powerful and important.

Debbie felt her skin crawl as John's arms invaded her space. You creep, she thought. You crawl out of that slut's bed and then you hug me. What next? You want sex? Oh Deb, I'm horny. Like a little boy. She was fortunate John had such a tight grip on her because his next words hit her like a sledge hammer. Blow after blow rained down on her, making her soul stagger under the onslaught. She couldn't believe what she was hearing, what he was saying......

"Debbie, I love you and I always will love you but I'm not in love with you, I've found someone else, oh she is beautiful and warm and loving and I need her and please be happy for me, I'm so happy" John's mouth rapid fired the bullets that tore Debbie's heart into shreds. He didn't know why he was blurting this out but he couldn't stop. It was like a floodgate opening, all the lies and deceit of the past few months being expunged by the simple act of confession. The catholic upbringing he had lived through until he met Debbie and left home had taught him confession was good for the soul and they were right. He was euphoric, ecstatic, relieved, sure he would work things out with Debbie and she would understand.

"I'll still look after you Deb, I've set up an allowance for you and you can keep this house and your car. We'll still be friends and go to dinner and I still want to be able to ring you and see how you are..."

Debbie pushed him away and took a step back. She wanted to slap his face but her arm refused to move. Her face contorted into a medusa like mask that only needed the serpents to finish the image of sheer hatred and loathing. She gave him a look of disgust and repulsion that stopped him in mid sentence. Even in the state she was in she recognised he was dumbstruck at how reviled she was at his news.

"You. Bastard. You. Fucking. Bastard!" Each word spat itself out of a mouth twisted with anger into a jagged tooth framed hole of hatred. "How dare you come into my home smelling of some slut's pussy and tell me to be happy for you. I slaved six nights a week so you could finish college and be somebody and you repay me with lies and deceit. Then you have the gall to think I'll be happy for you. You are a child!" The last word ended in a gob of spit that flew across the few inches that separated them and landed on his chin. "A child! You are not a man. A man would have the decency to be ashamed." She started to say more but couldn't get her words to come out. Her brain was racing with every nerve ending sending convoluted messages from one neuro-receptor to another. She tried to sort out the words from the thoughts and get the vocal chords to form them, but it was too much. Her sub-conscious took over and hit the safety valve it keeps for these times. Debbie feinted and fell to the floor, her body seeming to shrink in size with the enormity of the grief her soul was sifting through.

*****

"Pete, it's me".

"Hi. me" Pete replied, glad to hear his wife's voice for the first time in two days. "Where are you?"

"I'm staying at a girlfriend's place for a few days. I want to get my head together."

"Who, where?" Pete wanted to know where she was, if she needed help she should be at home with him. He was her husband.

"I'm at Sandy's flat, in Parramatta. You don't know her, she's a friend. I don't want you to know where I am. I need space. Time to think."

Pete felt very scared. He was losing his wife and he knew it. He'd known it for months but had refused to believe it. He wasn't going to give in without a fight, but he didn't want to crowd her. Give her some space and she'll be fine, he hoped. "O.K. Do you need anything?"

"No. I'm alright. I'll call you tomorrow. Bye." She hung up before he had a chance to say anything else. Pete stared at the phone in his hand. And sobbed. He hadn't cried for years, he wouldn't cry now. He pulled himself together and went out to sit with his dogs on the back step. His life was falling apart and he would not give in without a fight. He knew how to fight men. But how do you fight to regain love that is lost? Same as for men. Dirty. You fight with everything you have and you give no quarter until you win. He was not going to give up five feet from the finish line. He would see this through to the end. He had sworn to love and cherish Terri forsaking all others and he was a man of his word. It was old fashioned, he knew. But then he was an old fashioned kind of guy. A bit like John Wayne. Only the Duke was dead, long gone and buried.

*****

"He doesn't suspect a thing, alright." Terri was sick of John's whining. She knew Pete was totally unaware of what had really been going on. He was so trusting it had been almost too easy. Except that one time in bed...

"Well, I told Debbie, I had to." He was repeating himself. "Besides, it's better I've cleared things up with her. She was upset, as you would expect. But she'll realise I had to do it. And I will look after her, at least for a while." He knew Terri was sore about him still paying her bills, but he couldn't just cut her off. She'd go for his throat and divorce laws nowadays could ruin him. Of course he had discussed things with his solicitor. He was crazy about Terri, but he wasn't crazy enough to risk what he had built up.

"I can't believe you... what possessed you to?" Terri was so shocked he had told her everything she was virtually speechless. Of all the stupid... She pulled herself together and sat on the couch with a glass of wine. She drank a bottle or two every night, now. It was what got her through the evening. She also drank a bottle or two during the day. The long day sitting around the house too scared to go out in case Pete saw her. He would find them soon enough, she knew it was only a matter of time. Then what? John would need protecting. Pete would tear him apart. The house John had rented had a view of the harbour that added at least a couple of hundred a week to the rent. It was beautiful and such a change from Whalan. But it wasn't her home. Especially not as his best mate shared the place. Nice guy but still, not quite the love nest she had envisaged. A few bits of his furniture, some things they had bought together and the few clothes she had taken with her from home. She would have to tell Pete soon and get her share of their furniture and her personal effects. She was entitled to that, she had checked with her own solicitor. No blame divorce was what he called it. Adultery was a thing of the past, no longer a crime or even grounds to get more from the settlement. She wouldn't go for the house, but she wanted her share of what little equity they had in the place.

She had it all figured out. Plenty of time for that wandering around this luxury prison with water views. John had insisted she gave up her job pretty soon after they got together. That was understandable. She felt guilty taking money from him but she had bills to pay. She still had to get some money to Pete for their bills to keep up the facade she was working at the restaurant. She wondered how he would cope with two cars, a mortgage and the credit cards. Ah, well, too bad. His problem. She had enough worries of her own. She had to be tough and think of number one now.

Pete was suspicious at last. Time to break the faith and do a little intelligence gathering, he thought. He checked out the drawers she used in the bedroom, her wardrobe and the bathroom drawers. Nothing. What was he looking for, anyway? Anything that was out of the ordinary.

Here's something. A doctor's certificate from Penrith Hospital. The STD Clinic. STD? Sexually Transmitted Disease Clinic? The Jack Shack they had called it in the army. It was made out to a Stephanie Cowan, Terri's maiden name was Cowan, but Stephanie? She didn't have a sister, so? According to the chit, Stephanie was free of all strains of NSU, Syphilis, Gonorrhea, Hep A, B, C and HIV. Well that's a relief. But who is Stephanie and if Terri was using an alias, why a check up at the STD Clinic? Almost as if she was getting a health check for a brothel? NO! No way, no way Terri could do that. Pete knew his wife. She was soft with a tough streak but not that tough? And with her looks they would be rolling in money, so where was all the dough?

He started to notice what was missing. Her passport. Her birth certificate. Her credit cards, bank details, personal phone book, her resume. The phone rang. He walked into the study and picked up the handset. "Hello?"

"Mr Graham? Pete Graham?" A woman's voice, accented, American, New Jersey or Brooklyn. He felt the hair on the back of his neck stand on end.

"Yes, who am I speaking to?"

"My name is Debbie Tailor. My husband and your wife are having an affair."

Pete stared at the wall. He knew, in the clearest moment of understanding in his life, he knew. It was true. It made sense. His world collapsed and his heart went out to his wife. "Oh, Terri!"

CHAPTER 4

Pete stared across the table at Terri. She was beautiful, he had to give her that. She wore a tight top, tied at the front showing a firm, flat and tanned tummy. Her breasts stretched the material just enough to be sexy, not tarty. She had cut off denim shorts that advertised her legs, firm and tanned rather than long. But it was her face that still captured his heart. Framed by auburn curls and pure as the driven snow. She looked five years younger than the twenty nine and eleven months she actually was.

Terri took in the face of the man she had sworn to love over all others. She still loved him. But she was determined to go through with her plan. She knew it would hurt him but she had to do it. There had to be more to life than this little house and years of worrying how they'd pay the next bill. Pete was no oil painting. She hadn't fallen for his looks, rather his sense of humour and genuine love for her. John wasn't any better looking. And no better in bed, either. Worse probably, all selfish lust and no giving love. But he was going places. Pete was already there. He was at his destination. A nice little home, loving wife and good job. Comfortable. That was it. Pete was comfortable. But Terri didn't want comfortable. Not this kind, anyway. Comfortable to her was a lot more than a fibro house in a working class suburb, an old BMW and not enough money to shop till she dropped when the mood took her. And the mood took her a lot.

Pete could feel his life slipping away with each second of silence they shared. He was frightened of losing his life, his wife, everything he had. For once in his life he had felt, well... comfortable. Secure. A great wife, nice little house, good job. What was wrong with that? He'd spent enough time in one shit hole or another. Enough time living on the edge, pumped with adrenalin and fighting to survive. He had enjoyed every second but then he found Terri. He'd turned his back on the old life he had led and happily became a family man. Well, they had worked on the family part. Two miscarriages had taken their toll on Terri. But they could keep trying.

Three miscarriages, if you count the latest one. She hadn't told Pete about that one. It had happened right after she started at the parlour and just before she met John. Maybe that had been the catalyst. Up until then she would have been happy playing mum to Pete's children. But it hadn't happened and she must realise that was for a reason. So she could start her life anew. New man. New house. New future.

*****

They could start anew. Maybe move interstate. He'd get a job and they could make new friends. No one would have to know how it had been. How it had been so close. So close to falling apart.

Terri just shook her head and looked away from Pete. She couldn't meet his gaze, hearing not only his spoken protestations of love and change, but his wordless plea that shone from eyes wet with tears held back by sheer strength of will.

Pete asked her again. "Who is John, Terri? Tell me, I need to know."

*****

He'd found out earlier that day. Pete couldn't believe his ears. Debbie was telling him what he knew in his heart to be true. Every word. But he refused to believe it. If he refused to believe it enough it would go away and he would wake up and it would all be a horrible nightmare. She had proof. Credit card bills, phone bills, hotel receipts. Everything. Photo's from a P.I.'s report. He'd done enough of those himself to recognise a good one when he saw it.

Debbie had agreed to meet him at a friend's house. The friend now sat to one side nodding every now and then as if to add credibility to Debbie's story. As if she had discovered the truth herself rather than the private investigator. Obviously Debbie had confided in her so many times the story was well known to her, too. Pete heard it without really hearing it. It didn't matter about the details, anyway. The core of the tale was cruelly true and that was all that mattered.

He would call Terri and give her a chance to explain. He wouldn't yell, scream or get violent. What was the point. He loved her deeply, how could he get violent with the one person in the world he would gladly give his life for? After all, the guy hadn't forced her to have sex with him. She had led a six month life of deception of her own free will. It was just like boxing. Nobody dragged the fighters into the ring kicking and screaming. So why get violent? It would hardly bring his wife closer to him. No. He would stay calm and work it out. She would see the error of her ways and come back to him. No one had to know and they could get back on track.

*****

Terri looked at Pete and said simply, "You don't understand." She was right. Pete didn't understand but she wouldn't offer any explanation to help him understand. He was getting frustrated with her illogical handling of the situation but he kept his temper under control. Terri was frustrated that Pete didn't understand. She shouldn't have to explain, he should just know. A woman would know. Damn men!

*****

Terri was gone. Pete knew she wasn't coming back. He sat at his desk in the study and fell apart. Literally, fell apart. He moaned a soul wrenching keening sound that set his dogs howling to share the grief of their master. He staggered from doorframe to doorframe, supporting himself against the wall and ready to collapse from misery. He tore at his hair and cried unintelligible sobs of words and emotion, dribbling spit down his chin and racking his lungs with coughs of despair. His whole body was going into shut down mode to protect itself from harm. Only his tortured mind continued to plague his soul with pity. Terri was gone. His life was over.

*****

Terri could hardly drive the car as she hurried away from the life she had once led. The house, her garden, her things. Well, she'd come back for her stuff once Pete realised it was over. She would still get her share of the equity in the house and she would keep her car. Pete had his, she'd have hers. She'd be generous with their furniture. But there were quite a few things she would not walk away from. Nice things, presents from their families. She still cried as she drove. But she knew she would get over it. It had gone easier than she thought. Pete hadn't lost it, maybe he was too shocked. Thank God for that.

"I need space. Look, John is just a guy I met at work. He came out with me and three of the girls from work for a drink after we'd finished one night. Nothing happened. He has trouble with his wife. She's a looney. Mad. He just needed someone to talk to. Yes, it's a parlour but I'm just a receptionist, a hostess. Look, I need to be by myself for a while. I'm staying with a girl friend in the city for a few days. I'll call you. I promise."

That was what she had said to Pete. It was a load of crap, but it had given her the space she needed to get away. She had denied the story that Debbie had told him. Looked Pete in the eye and lied through her teeth. She had to. Otherwise he might have got angry and bashed her. She would call him soon and end it all properly. She had meant to when she called and said she was coming home to get some things, then he hit her with that "Who is John?" bullshit. So calm. As if he didn't want to rip her head off. "Who is John?" She had nearly wet herself with fear. Her stomach churned, her mouth went sweet and cold with adrenalin and her voice shook with the effort of keeping herself under control. Terri had almost ran from the house screaming, but she had kept control. She was proud of herself for that. It meant she was changing, getting a grip and taking charge. It might have been better if he had lost it. Got it over and done with. Maybe a little smack so she could pull an Apprehended Violence Order on him. She didn't want him in gaol or hurt, just needed some space to get her life back on track.

*****

The light coming through the window decided it was fed up with illuminating the gloom of Nikki's life and called it a night. Left alone at last, Nikki reached for the scotch and poured a small one. It sat in the cut glass tumbler that had been a present the first time she had been a punching bag and looked at her wistfully. Sure of its fate, the amber liquid was stoic as it awaited the final journey to her liver. At least there it would have the chance to avenge itself. Nikki envied the scotch as she picked up the glass and raised it to her lips. She had no-one to avenge herself on. Don's kids? His ex-wife? The makers of the car? The hose company? Noxious gases in general?

The odour of the fermented grains made her cringe and sit the glass down with a shudder that oscillated from her shoulders to her knees. It would have reached her feet only she had her legs crossed and it died a natural death within sight of it's goal. "No!" Nikki spoke the word out loud. "NO!" she repeated, louder and with more feeling. She would not give in and join Don in the pit of pathetic self sorrow that had swallowed up the man and his dreams. She ejected the scotch from the glass into the sink, tossing his relatives still accommodated in the bottle into the garbage bin with just as little ceremony. She stood, arms akimbo and surveyed the kitchen-dining room with contempt. She had let things slip, hadn't she.

The clean-up took hours, hours in which she commuted her self esteem from the outer suburb of self pity to the inner-city world of trendy high density housing. She renovated and remodeled her life as she washed the dishes of despair her days of morose indulgence had allowed to build up in the sink. Bitterness and anger aimed without only damaged within. She knew that, yet had still fallen prey to its easy invasion of her life. Her LIFE. As in get one, Nikki. Don was dead and nothing would either bring him back or make him sorry for what he had left behind. The only way he would win was if she followed him into the pit. And she had two reasons for living. Two examples of added value to her brief appearance on life's stage.

The children would be coming home from their father's in an hour or so. Seeing her shift into higher gear, the light had accelerated its return while she cleaned away the detritus of her fall from grace. No way would they find their mother still in her night gown and sodden with booze. Nikki turned on the shower and purged the madness from her skin that had very nearly seeped into every fibre of her being. She scrubbed away the stink of defeat and glowed with the victory of beating Don's challenge to waste herself as he had done. A new Nikki emerged from the shower and cast a critical eye over her late thirties body. Not bad. Not bad if she did say so herself. And who else could have disagreed since she was very much alone in the bathroom they had planned together when the future seemed so bright and untarnished. A few lines, a little sag here and there, but still, not too bad all told. She chose her brightest dress and tied back her hair with her favourite scarf. Makeup and cologne completed an ensemble her family had not seen for some time as she heard the car pull into the driveway. The Donald R. Henderson Memorial Driveway. Screw him. Nikki had her life back and Donald R. Henderson could rot in his grave for all she cared.

*****

Pete knew it was bullshit. A guy she met at work. Just a receptionist. He knew it was crap. But Christ he wanted to believe it. She just sat there, looking him in the eye and filling his head with utter crap. He felt like shaking her until she told the truth but he didn't want to face the truth. He knew the truth and it hurt too much. Little bits at a time. He couldn't absorb the enormity of it all in one go. So he let her carry on with the charade and walk out of the door and out of his life. Gone. Shit!

*****

"I'm so sorry, Pete. I love my husband and I want him back. But your, I'm sorry, hussy of a wife has cast a spell over him." Debbie was consoling Pete. Sub-consciously, she was loving every minute, every second of his obvious pain. Talk about wearing your heart on your sleeve. This guy was dying here. Right in front of her. She didn't know why she was so excited, so turned on, juiced up. This was the worst thing in her life, his too. Yet she was enjoying it. Debbie was a smart lady, but she didn't know about schardenfreund. A German term for feeling elated at someone else's bad news. It was really just a feeling of relief that it was their grief and not yours. A feeling most of us have had and felt guilty for. Why should we be secretly delighted at a friend's misfortune? Simply because our primal survival instincts are still with us and kick in at times like those, making us revel at being alive and unhurt.

*****

Pete knew she must be loving every minute of this. At last she was striking back at the woman who stole her husband. Not face to face, but the next best way. Through him. It all made sense now. The pieces of the puzzle were coming together with alarming rapidity. Incidents and conversations that had left him puzzled now made complete sense. He would confront Terri. But he would stay calm. Give her a chance to tell him her version of these grubby events. Deny it, he almost said. Deny it he almost willed.

*****

Debbie was worried. She had seen the thousand yard stare in Pete Graham's eyes when he left her friend's house. He had said he would confront his wife. Pete Graham was not a man she would like to have after her. Jack Regan had been right. John had picked on the wrong guy if this fella decided to get even. A part of her was also worried for Terri, too. But only a little part and not for long. Screw that young, beautiful bitch. And screw you John. You got it coming to you.

*****

Pete waved at Debbie to sit down and join him at the cafe table he'd waited at for the past half hour. "Sorry I'm late" Debbie gasped, still huffing from the run to the cafe in the rain. "Had to park miles away."

"It's O.K." Pete replied. "I'll get the waitress over, just coffee?" Debbie nodded as she arranged herself around the chair. Handbag on the table, umbrella on the vacant seat to her left, coat on the seat to her right. By the time Pete had caught the waitresses eye and ordered another coffee, Debbie was settled.

"So where do you think they are living?" she asked.

"Mosman."

"Mosman? How do you know?"

Pete explained how he had checked his wife's credit card bill and noticed two entries for a service station in Mosman. Different days, same place. There was another entry for a different servo, but also in the same street. Probably the closest place to home. He had grabbed a street directory and located the service stations. From the addresses in the yellow pages he knew them to be virtually opposite each other. So she had to use one coming and the other going. One entry coincided with before her last visit to their home, so that servo was the going. This meant she lived east of the two. He'd drawn a circle of about two kilometres radius using the servo's as the datum, then focused on the half of the circle to the east. Most of the area was harbour, so he had effectively narrowed down the search area to half a dozen or so streets. These he had listed for Debbie to look at and see if she recognised any of them. He had also checked the numbers on her mobile phone bill, which was in his name and he was responsible for the outstanding debt. One number that appeared three times belonged to a Sam somebody. He checked the number through his Phone Disc CD Rom and came up with a name and address. The Phone Disc allowed searching via street, name, post code, business type and number.

"Do you know a Sam White, or S. White of 34 Bella Vista Street, Mosman?" he asked her.

"Sammy." Debbie was stunned. The term 'knocked me down with a feather' went through her mind. "Do I know him? He's one of our oldest friends. John and him went through college together. Do you think they are staying with Sam?" If they were then Debbie felt betrayed. Sam had become her friend as much as John's. At least she thought he had. Sam!

"Well, there's one way to find out. Let's go over there and knock on the door." Pete offered.

Then what? Smack him in the mouth? Pointless. The scumbag was just getting his end away. Just because he was a gutless slime ball who screwed other men's wives didn't erase the fact the other man's wife had let him do it. No. More like find out who was going to make the payments on her car, her phone, the mortgage. Boring day to day minutiae of the reality of life.

"Yes!" Debbie's eyes grew wide with the excitement generated by the thought of confronting John and his slut in their love nest. Love nest. Den of depravity and disgust, more like it. "We'll knock on the door and tell them just what we think of them."

Boy, Pete thought, that'll bring them back. Not! What else could he do? "O.K., we'll go and have a scout around. Do a recce as we used to say in the army. If we think there is any point in confronting them, we'll do it."

"Are you going to hit him?" Debbie held her breath for the reply.

"I don't know." And Pete was right. He didn't know. He knew he wanted to, but whether he would or not was another matter. He'd have to see when the time came.

*****

"There's her car!" Pete pointed to the vehicle, his voice rising just slightly with the excitement. He felt a little nauseous, tense and anticipatory. It was almost like the old days. But he was in the right and he was in charge. Now he was going into battle he felt better than he had for the past half a year. At last he was taking action.

The car was parked in a parallel street. Maybe parking had been tough when she got back, maybe she was taking precautions. If that was the case then it showed her guilt. But he knew she was guilty. He still tried to cling to the vague hope she had been telling the truth about staying with a girlfriend, but he knew he was only trying to fool himself. She was in that house. With him. Right now.

40

"We'll park up the street and approach on foot. I'll scout around a bit before we knock on the door." Debbie simply nodded her agreement. She was pretty pumped up too. She quite liked the feeling, if the truth were known. She felt more alive than she had for ages. She walked behind Pete as he silently closed in with the house. He was remarkably quiet for such a big guy, but then he had been a commando or something, hadn't he?

Pete signaled for her to wait by the gate. He opened the gate without making a sound and walked on the grass next to the path. He could see shadows through the window. The curtains were drawn but there was definitely movement at the station. There was a dark alley up the side of the house, presumably to the rear yard. He held off in case they had a dog, or he set a neighbours dog off. Pete walked back around to the front and approached the door. He knocked loudly two or three times then waited. The shadows had frozen on the other side of the curtains the second he had knocked. He sensed rather than heard a whispered conversation from within. Then the light he could see beyond the frosted glass set in the front door went out. He knocked again and repeated the waiting and listening act. Nothing. He banged louder and called out to the silent occupants.

"Terri. I know you are in there. Please come to the door. We need to talk."

The only reply was a light scuffling sound from inside the house. Then nothing. He banged again and repeated his message, forcing himself to remain calm and to sound reasonable. Even though he had every right to not be reasonable. His wife was inside that house with a man who had no scruples, no moral courage or fibre. He had every right to kick the damn door off its hinges and rip the place and the occupants into tiny pieces. But that wouldn't make Terri love him again. Nor would it pay the bloody bills. Pete remembered a sign that had hung in his C.O.'s office when he was in the army. It was a reminder to keep the objective in sight at all times. It went something like: "When you're up to your ass in alligators, try to remember the reason you are there is to drain the damned swamp." Good advice and timely in recollection, he thought.

Pete tried the knock and call once more. No answer. He remembered something else from his army days. If you are going to do it, don't piss about. Get in, get it done and get the hell out. Time to play hard.

CHAPTER 5

The door crashed back into the hall from the force of the kick. It had hardly begun its return swing, ricocheting off the wall and obeying one of Newton's various laws as Pete exploded through the doorway and pounded down the hall. He sensed rather than saw two people in the living room to his right and immediately changed course. He stopped at the entrance to the room and took in the vision of his wife and another man frozen in fear at his sudden appearance.

Terri screamed and took a pace forward, putting herself between her husband and the man she had betrayed him for. Even in the heat of the moment, Pete applauded her courage, simultaneously sickened by the cringing cowardice of the man who sheltered behind her skirts.

"PETE!" Terri cried. "Don't!" Terri's terror stricken voice pleaded and commanded at the same time.

"Don't what?" asked Pete. "Don't rip his fucking heart out or don't slap the living shit out of you? Whore!" If Pete could have seen himself at that moment he would have recognised the combat ready slight crouch, the tense muscles quivering in anticipation of action. Instead his vision had narrowed so all he saw in any detail was his wife standing a few feet in front of him, everything else a peripheral blur.

"Don't do anything. Get out! You have no right..." Terri's fear caused her words to taper off into the ether as Pete took a half step toward the pair. He reached out and deftly pushed his wife to one side making her trip and fall into a sofa straight out of a Vogue Living magazine. John looked up and into the eyes of the man he had cuckolded. At that point he sensed his life was hanging by a thread. Cold, icy fear gripped his stomach, his mouth went dry and his throat swelled so he couldn't even utter a cry for help if his life depended on it. And at that precise moment his life did depend on more than just a cry for help. He needed the real, tangible, two large coppers kind of help. And he knew he wasn't going to get it.

Pete was close enough to smite the man who had ripped apart his life and set him on the path of vengeance. He felt his right hand tremble with kinetic power stored ready to explode upwards and smash the heel of his palm into the face of the man in front of him. Man? Pete didn't think of him as a man. To him a man didn't take another man's wife, steal her heart and conscience with a handful of money and a fuck full of promises. A man didn't abandon his own woman just because he was ready for a newer model. A wife wasn't a car or a stereo, but a partner in life.

Pete looked again at the man who had changed his life forever, saw clearly the lines of fear and terror on his face, etched with the chisel of money and privilege. Sanded smooth with the ease of buying whatever his twisted little heart desired and damn the cost to the poor bastards who fell by the way. He half turned his head to see his wife still sprawled on the sofa, staring intently as the drama of disgust and loathing played itself out in three acts in his mind. Looking back at John he knew he would not lower himself to strike this worm. He wasn't worth it, simple as that. Pete knew he wouldn't even raise a hand to defend himself. It would be like beating a submissive dog. And where was the satisfaction in that?

Debbie got to the living room door just as Pete turned away in utter disgust. She looked in his eyes and saw the palette of emotions mix into one shapeless mélange of abstract pain. Denied the primal lust quenching of defeating his rival in battle, Pete could only walk away with what shreds of his dignity she had left untattered. He brushed past Debbie as she shrank from the doorway and made room for his exit. She looked at last upon the face of the woman who had taken her life and turned it into a living hell of self doubt and despair. As Terri stood up from the sofa she crossed the room and slapped Terri across the face with a sound that made John jump in his worthless skin. "SLUT!" she spat, then turned on John. "Bastard!" she said but with less venom that all in the room registered. It was clear who she really blamed for her husband's infidelity. Herself. For succumbing to natures' law of gravity and ageing.

Terri and John stood silently as Debbie followed Pete out of the room, down the hall and into the street. Recovering first, Terri reached a hand to sooth the sting of the blow as she stepped towards John and took him in her arms. She had never been slapped before and she vowed she would never feel such pain again. John shrunk into her grasp and started to shake with the relief of his narrow escape. He had seen a side of himself he did not like, but had always known he possessed. Only he knew how close he had come to pissing himself in abject terror.

*****

"I thought when you kicked the door in you were going to kill them both." Debbie said as they drove away.

"So did I" Pete replied. "I just couldn't do it. He wasn't worth the effort, let alone the cost." Pete had really known that all along, but he had had to go there and see the scumbag for himself. See what his wife had torn his heart in two for. The nice house, the harbour views, the money on tap to shop without having to count the pennies. And for all that she has cut herself off from his family, her family. Well, not for long. Blood, after all, is thicker than water. Not that her family ever had much to do with them. Too wound up in their own personal problems. Her father had been an adulterer, throwing money around like water. But only to wet other women whilst her mother did her best to bring the two children up on the little housekeeping he hadn't kept for himself. She was too involved in her own new relationship to really worry about anyone but herself. Even Terri's brother was off looking after number one.

Debbie saw again in her mind the young, beautiful whore who had tempted her man from the straight and narrow path of familiarity and comfortable married life. She blamed herself for being too old for him, not pretty enough, not exciting enough. Hadn't she always done whatever he wanted? If he came home and said "Dee, I'm horny, will you give me some special kisses?" didn't she always go down there and do it for him? Never said no. Anything his little heart desired, she had done for him. And it wasn't enough because she had started out thirteen years behind the eight ball. She had worried this day would come ever since she first fell for him. Nineteen and still a virgin. It had been exciting for him then, doing it with an older woman. But older women just keep getting older whilst men age with dignity and increasing sex appeal. Why else would Hollywood have fifty plus year olds scoring twenty something love interests? Art imitating life? Debbie looked out of the window so Pete could not see the tear rippling over the crows foot at the corner of her eye.

Pete looked across at Debbie and felt her pain, almost like a radioactive wave of hurt pulsing with every heartbeat. He knew what she was thinking. For her it was years. For Pete, dollars. Dollars and all that money could buy. Not the intangibles, the immaterial, the abstract things that he placed above the cars, houses, holidays and share portfolio's. But all the things Terri craved and he hadn't been able to supply, like offerings on the altar of abundance and consumerism. One day he would realise it had been destined to end as it did, doomed from the start as his sweet young wife grew and changed. Changed from wanting the security of a man who would love and protect her to the need for money and power, position and wealth. Bloody Shakespearean, it was. Classic tale of lust and betrayal only he was living it, not reading about it.

*****

Terri watched as John repaired the lock as best the damage would allow, mumbling something about getting it fixed properly in the morning, suing Pete, calling the police, taking out an apprehended violence order and calling his lawyer. All in one half sentence. Yes, she thought. You'd call the police and sue his arse because then someone else would have to take him in, face him in court and you could sit safely in your office high above the reality of life and think how brave you were to press charges. She had no misconceptions about her lover, now. She couldn't understand it but part of her had wanted Pete to break him in two. Those thoughts quickly dissolved as she started to plan how to turn this to her advantage. John would be even more puttylike in her sculptor's hands, now. She would pull herself together, take John to bed and restore some of his lost manhood in the best way she knew how and then turn the shit into gold. More gold. After all. That was what this had been all about right from the start.

*****

The door closed and the two appointed good Samaritans walked into the living room, pausing embarrassedly as they waited for Nikki to indicate where they should sit. She had a hard time deciding if they actually could sit, what with all the debris from the move littering the room. Strewn was the word that came to her mind as she ushered the pair out onto the balcony. It was a big balcony, big enough for the parties they had planned to share together over the coming years. House warming, birthdays, Christmas, new years, wedding anniversaries. Parties that would now be for the same reasons, just not all the original cast would be present.

The man and the woman sat down at the garden table and both looked at Nikki at the same time, almost as if their concentrated gaze would make everything alright. Mumbling their acceptance to the offer of refreshment gave them a few more minutes to compose themselves before going about the Lord's work. As Nikki set down the coffee cups and perched herself on the edge of a chair, ready to flee should the need arise, the man opened his mouth to speak. Typically, the woman, introduced as his 'good wife', an archaic oxymoron in Nikki's mind, beat him to it.

"Firstly, all of us at the church were very sorry to hear about your loss. You did know Don was Born Again Pentecostal?" she asked, making it sound like a disease he had bravely suffered under silently for many years.

"Yes, but it didn't bother me." Nikki replied, without thinking then almost put her hand to her mouth as she realised how that sounded.

"Then he hasn't come into your life, yet?" The man, finding his voice, said.

"Who?" Nikki asked rather vaguely.

"Why Our Lord, Jesus Christ!" The woman made it sound like everyone in the world bar Nikki knew who the man had meant. Everyone on the balcony at least since the three of them were alone, the children being at school.

"Oh, sorry. No. Well,... you see I am Agnostic, a fence sitter you might say."

The man and woman exchanged looks that were visual cliché's, confirming Nikki's decision to get them off her balcony, out of her house and out of her life as fast as decency and good manners allowed.

"Don had found the Lord some time ago. He was always at service, until a year or so ago. Fell from the path and..." he let the rest hang. Nikki knew what he was implying. It was about a year ago she had met him. He had mentioned religion to her once or twice at first but gave up after she made it patently clear that her beliefs were private and personal, something she kept to herself and would appreciate he did the same. He had been a bit moody after that for a day or so but she had felt it important to let him know where she stood as early in their relationship as possible. After that he never mentioned the subject again and stopped going to church, not that she had wanted him to.

"Yes, we feel we may have been able to prevent this tragedy if we had only kept in better contact with him. We all blame ourselves for this." The woman continued, but you could see she didn't blame herself at all. Neither did he. Both of them looked at Nikki so that she, too, knew who was really to blame. And am I? Nikki asked herself. Did my denial of his spiritual needs compound the pain and torment he was already suffering? Would he have snapped out of whatever it was that caused him to do such a thing if he had received better guidance, help or at least a sympathetic ear from his fellow parishioners? Nikki reflected on that, even as she resented the huge guilt trip the man and woman had just dispatched her on. They were still talking as she divided her mind so half of her could take in what the two were saying and the other half could be alone and think. Something women can do that men can't. Multi tasking, her latest self help book called it.

*****

The morning after the night before, as they say, found Pete still none the wiser about the cold facts of life regarding such unromantic concepts such as mortgage payments, car payments, credit cards, electricity bills etc. He had been copping the lot for some time now, Terri hadn't contributed a penny for months. She had made the last payment on her car, but then she was driving it and so she should pay for it. But Pete had been struggling to make ends meet. If she had been such a high class call girl, where was all the money? His mind shot off on a debate of the term high class used in conjunction with call girl. Prostitute. Hooker. Whore. Worker. Lady of ill repute. Brothel, bordello, cat house, knocking shop, massage parlour. Words, just words. But words were what we humans used to organise and control our thoughts, our lives. Without words, simply labels recognised and accepted by all to mean the same thing, we had no order. No way of communicating beyond grunts and pointing, or drawing pictures. Fine until you wanted to communicate abstract concepts like love, loyalty, fidelity, honesty.

Pete was in a kind of spousal denial, post traumatic shock for the newly abandoned male. He could not believe his Terri would leave him. Actually leave him. Him. Her. It just couldn't be true. It was a dream, a waking dream and yet, so real. So gut wrenchingly real. So real the tears would come and go without conscious effort or realisation until he found himself sniffing and sucking up snot and salt. How's the big, tough commando now? he derisively asked his reflection. He looked again at the face he saw in the mirror and asked his face why? Why him? Why her? Why?

The face stared back with the same tortured look he knew was on his face. Of course it would, it's my bloody face. He half laughed, half cried at his own stupid revelation and looked again in the mirror. The eyes are the windows to the soul, he'd once read. Well these windows are fogged up. Fogged up and full of bull shit tears for a woman who chose another man over him. Him. Her. Christ!

Pete wanted to know. His fragile male ego, like any man's, demanded he know. What did she see in that scumbag? Was he better looking to her? Was he better in bed than Pete was? Did he have a bigger dick? Pete couldn't even consider him a man. No man as Pete classified the term, would screw another man's wife. No man would hide behind a woman to avoid the smack in the mouth he would surely know he had coming to him? Pete was no rocket scientist, but he wasn't thick, either. Money. Money is power. Simple as that. She wanted his money. With money she had the power to do whatever she wanted. Whenever she wanted.

He had tried to give her that power. When she moved in to his flat seven years ago he had been debt free. Owned his car, no debts, own furniture, good job. Within six months he had a new car and a payment book to go with it. They had been on a holiday overseas to Thailand. She had shopped till she dropped, all on plastic. His furniture was a thing of the past. All new stuff. New flat, too. Closer in to the city and twice the rent. Finally he had been able to move out west where they could afford to buy. Stop renting. Dead money. Yada yada yada. At first she had been rapt. Spent thousands on the garden. Do you know how much a rose bush can set you back? New carpets, new kitchen, new car. The list went on and on, almost like an FBI profiler reporting on the likely nature of a serial killer. Only this woman was a serial shopper.

So what happens when John-boy runs out of dough? That Debbie of his was going to clean him out. Pete was glad she was on his side. Then what mister big dick? Terri will dump you and move on, work her way up the corporate ladder to the guy whose company she really wants to keep. The company, lock, stock and shareholdings. Little consolation for a man who still loved his wife. Loved her with the passion only the loser of something can feel for the lost love. And why not? Two days ago he still believed she was just shitty with him for snoring or not washing the dishes or not making enough money. It's like when someone you love dies. You don't suddenly stop holding them in your arms just because the doctor declares life extinct. The cooling collection of hydrogen and helium and a few other chemicals you cradle to your heart was, a breath before, someone you loved. Loved you. Lived. Breathed. Laughed, sang, loved, hated, cried, pissed, shat. Pete took another swallow from the bourbon he was using to make himself this morosely poetic and shook his head. It didn't work. The thoughts and emotions danced around and around, laughing, calling him names. Loser. Couldn't keep her, could you? Too rich for your blood, hey stud. Bet he's not crying now. No, he'll be getting your bit, won't he.

Funny how men always think of the sexual side of things first. Women worry about the loss of love and feelings. Men, the loss of a good bit of stuff on a regular basis. But Pete knew she meant more than that to him. Yes, there was the thing about some bloke doing his missus. But it takes two to tango. She must have wanted it too. Nobody forced her into prostitution. The balanced, mature Pete reasoned the bloke was just doing what blokes do. How can you really blame him? Pete would have given up everything for her too. But then he wasn't married when he met her, was he? He didn't meet her at the end of a Gold Visa card, did he? Being able to communicate abstract concepts meant man first had to be able to think in abstract terms. There was a difference. A difference between winning a woman's promise to be his alone through force of personality and buying it like any other commodity. A difference between looking and touching, crossing the line from coveting your neighbours wife to shagging the arse off her.

He put down his empty glass and reached for the phone. He had the number of the house she was at. This was stupid. They had to talk, sort things out. Do something.

*****

Terri put the phone down and walked to the fridge to top up her wine glass. The young constable had been very nice, very understanding. He understood she was just letting the police know, in case her husband came around again and decided to finish the job. No, she didn't want to press charges for last night, but yes, she would call if she felt in danger. She didn't want to take out an AVO on Pete, but he had scared the daylights out of her, bursting in like he did. To be expected, she figured. Why couldn't he just accept it was over and let her go.

Terri used the female interpretation of logic, which is just as valid as the male kind, only lacking in any recognised scientific basis, which meant she could see things so clearly. If only Pete could see it the same way. Then he would simply accept that things had changed and move on. The few close friends she had confided in had all agreed with her. Since they only had her version of events and had both abandoned their previous spouse it was understandable they would lend some form of credence and respectability to their own infidelity by supporting hers. Almost like sneaking a smoke in the toilets at school. If you all did it then it was alright, wasn't it?

Terri had overcome her qualms and misgivings months ago. About the time she decided to put a price on her virtue, for want of a better term. She had rationalised everything in her own mind then, so by now she was convinced she was quite within her rights to proceed as planned. Her mind had erased all but the last few shards of shame her betrayal had thrown up. It really hadn't taken that much, either. Once she was on the roller coaster of lies and deceit, the ride became easier. More enjoyable. Not so scary.

The ringing of the phone made her jump. She looked at the instrument as if by sheer intuition she could deduce who was on the other end of the line. Maybe it was John? Checking to see if she was okay? Perhaps the young constable had forgotten something for his report? Pete? No. Surely he wouldn't have the number? But then he had found the house and she was sure he wouldn't be able to do that. Not as quickly as he had. The phone gave another ring, tired of waiting to be picked up. Terri reached out and slowly put the hand piece to her ear.

"Terri?" was all she heard before she slammed the handset down and reached, trembling, for her wine.

CHAPTER 6

Pete knocked on the door he had kicked in only a few hours before. He was back at her house trying to sort out the details of who was paying what. He knocked again, knowing she wouldn't answer. He'd tried to ring and let her know he was coming around but the phone was constantly engaged, or off the hook.

He walked around the side of the house and peered in through the French windows at the rear. No sign of movement. Back at the front he knocked again, convinced she was there but refusing to answer. Giving up he went back to his car to write her a note and slip it under the door. He thought back to his phone call to John a few hours ago when he had given up listening to her busy signal.

"Listen, I just need to speak to my wife to sort out who is paying for the mortgage, the car, the bills and so on." he had said, trying to sound reasonable.

"Well," came back the snotty reply in an obviously affected Lower North Shore English Accent. "You will have to ring her at home. Its nothing to do with me, your financial troubles."

Pete could have reached down the line and throttled him. "It is, as a matter of fact. If she wasn't off screwing you she would have been contributing to our mutual debts, mate."

"None of my business. I am not responsible for these things." he replied, infuriating Pete further.

"Look, mate, you think your money and power means you can screw your way through life while screwing the lives of others, but let me tell you." He paused for effect, but not for too long in case the swine hung up. " Every thing you do has an effect on someone else and you will have to pay for your fun, one way or another."

"Are you threatening me?" His imperious tone lacked a little of the previous arrogance he had projected through the phone line.

"I don't threaten." Pete's voice actually dropped in volume as he spoke. "I just take action."

"Well, I have it on the best legal advice available that there isn't anything you can do to me. There is no law of adultery in this state, anymore." The last word spoken almost as an afterthought but with poorly disguised relief.

"I'm not talking suing you, fuck knuckle. I just want to know where the next car payment is coming from. I can't get my wife to pick up the phone and it occurred to me she might be there with you. It might be a game to you, but it's my bloody life we're talking about here."

"That is your problem, not mine. She's not here and besides, my relationship with your wife is of no consequence."

Pete couldn't believe his ears. What, no consequence to him? To Pete? It bloody was of consequence. "Yeah." snarled Pete at the handset, "just remember one thing, mate." He paused and could hear the other man's breathing stop and hold in anticipation. "Every time you kiss my wife you've got my cock in your mouth!" And with that Pete had hung up and headed for his car. As he was doing now. Only now he was going to write a letter that hopefully his wife would read, realise he meant her no harm and call him so they could work something out.

*****

He was sitting behind the wheel, half way through what was turning out to be a long letter when he saw the first movement out of the norm on the quiet, upper class street. Glancing in the rear view mirror as some movement caused a change in the light and thus attracted his attention, he saw a plain white Commodore pull in to the kerb a hundred yards or so behind him. He checked the side mirror and saw a man, obviously a plain clothes cop, jump out of the car and duck into a block of flats. The driver locked the car and followed. Pete looked to his front and saw another unmarked police car pull in at the bottom of the street. He was trapped.

So what? He knew they were cops, knew it had to be him they were after. But why? He hadn't done anything wrong. If they were going to hit him for last night they would have dragged him out of bed this morning. No. She must have called them when he knocked. The time frame was about right. Good response in these upmarket areas. You wouldn't see hide nor hair of them for over forty minutes if this was home.

Another police car, a marked paddy wagon, pulled in behind him. At the same time a patrol car turned in to the street in front of him and parked across the street from the unmarked car, facing the wrong way. So, these guys mean business. He put down the half finished letter and his pen and wound up the window of the truck. Taking the keys from the ignition, he slowly opened the door and got out. Pointless running, he was surrounded. Besides, he'd done nothing wrong, committed no crime. Why should he run?

He used the shiny paintwork on the side of the truck to monitor the progress of the two officers sneaking up behind him. The marked patrol car had disgorged two rather large constables who were adjusting their equipment belts and starting to move towards him. The man and woman in the front unmarked car also got out, but hung back a little from the two uniforms. The pair in the paddy wagon behind him remained in their seats, the engine probably running but too far away for Pete to hear.

Pete knew this was looking serious. These cops weren't messing around. They knew their business and that is what they meant. The two plain clothes guys on the other side of the truck were now parallel with the vehicle and no longer reflecting off the paint, but Pete could see them through the truck's side windows. He slowly walked into the middle of the quiet street and raised his arms, hands open and fingers outstretched to show he was unarmed.

"Gentlemen!" he called out. "What seems to be the problem?" he kept his voice calm and even, glad he had made the first contact, trying to maintain some kind of initiative on the events about to unfold. He didn't want the cops to get carried away, especially as two of them had their side arms drawn and the other four had their PR24 batons in hand. Pete had trained with the PR24, side handle baton, as preferred by nine out of ten LAPD cops when battering minority motorists into oblivion. He preferred the straight KB28, easier to train, use and hang onto, but the PR24's looked more business like.

One of the plain clothes cops put his revolver away in a holster under his loose shirt and behind his back and approached Pete. "Sir" he said with a definite American accent, " please keep your hands up and don't move".

Pete did as he was told and asked again what the problem was.

"Sir, do not say anything, stand there with your hands out and do not move" the cop repeated. By this time he was at Pete's side and very quickly reached down to his pocket and snatched up Pete's Spyderco Pocket Clipit. Pete could have kicked himself. He always carried the little knife for cutting string and boxes at work and had forgotten it was there. Immediately he thought of the machete in the truck, amongst his camping gear that hadn't been cleaned out since his last trip away. Then he remembered the expandable baton and knuckledusters he carried in the console, just in case. Things were not looking good for Pete. If the cops found them, he was screwed. The machete he could explain, the other two were both prohibited articles and carried a couple of years gaol time each. Bugger.

"Knife." the American cop called to his team as he deftly put it in a back pocket of his jeans. He stepped behind Pete and quickly but expertly searched him for more weapons. Pete knew better than to try and explain the knife right at that moment. Keep your mouth shut and let these guys do their thing. Once they knew you were harmless you would get more out of them. Right now, they didn't know who or what they were up against except he had a knife on him when they searched him. Things were going from bad to worse very quickly for Pete.

"Move over there, to the side of the road, Sir" the American cop directed Pete onto the pavement across the street from the house. Too far away to do any harm and away from his truck. The two uniforms from the paddy wagon got out of their vehicle and went into the house, followed by the man and woman plain clothes cops. The American, his partner and the two big blokes from the patrol car formed a loose ring around Pete.

"Am I under arrest, constable?" Pete asked.

"No sir" the American replied.

"In that case, I would like to leave now, thank you". Pete figured it was worth a try.

"If you try to walk away, then I will arrest you" came the reply.

"In that case," said Pete, looking at his watch, "I will consider myself under arrest as at one thirty pee em"

"Please yourself" came the droll reply, obviously the cop wasn't worried about any false arrest suits.

"Why am I being held here against my will?" Pete tried again.

"We need to sort out this situation and you are helping us with our inquiries"

Pete just looked at the four cops surrounding him and knew it was useless to argue. He figured he could explain the knife, even the machete. But if they searched the truck and found the baton and knuckle dusters........ He was, in a word, fucked!

*****

The phone call had made Terri sit down and cry for nearly half an hour before she could even think of doing anything more. She had managed to throw the handset off the hook to stop any more calls coming in. John would call her on her mobile, anyway. She felt sick. Her stomach churned with the finality of the path she had chosen to tread. She knew she had to go on with it, see it through to the bitter end. But what would that end be? If only she could turn back the clock and start all over again. No! It was useless. What will be, will be. She had made her bed and now she must lie in it. Even if the sheets were rumpled and soiled with the stains of shame and greed.

Terri reviewed her life to date. From when she had made the decision to go on the game to this very moment in time. It had all happened too fast, gotten out of control. Too late now to change anything. She could only hope that time would heal all wounds. Two, three years from now she would be divorced from Pete and living a new life. One of abundance and security with no worries about the future. She could shop when she wanted, buy whatever she wanted. Live in a nice house in a good suburb. The right address. She deserved it. She was beautiful, she should have the best. Not some two bit fibro dump in the middle of a bunch of dole bludgers and single mothers.

Feeding her anger with how hard done by she had been made her feel better, more confidant. She transferred her guilt and anger, her fear and her shame onto Pete. After all, he had put her in this situation. If only he had wanted more, worked harder. It was all his fault. He deserved whatever he got. Even distraught as she was, Terri couldn't convince herself of this totally. Just enough to allow her to think of something else. Anything other than the gnawing fear, eating at her guts.

It was all so confusing. She still loved Pete. Loved? Love? But not IN LOVE. Her mind was jumping all over the place but she knew exactly what she meant. The love was more like a sentimental comfort zone rather than a passion. Not that she felt passion for John. There had been passionate moments, sure. Raunchy sex does get very passionate. But that was the result of it being illicit, extramarital and novel rather than particularly good sex.

It wasn't the sex, anyway. John was no better in bed than Pete, no better looking, either. Most men look pretty stupid with their clothes off, anyway. And the hunks who did look good weren't attractive enough mentally. Didn't have the power men like John had. Didn't have the drive, the money. Pete had the power, but not the drive or the money. He had so much potential and he was happy plodding along, day to day. Pity.

Terri had calmed down after the police said they were arresting Pete and taking him away. She signed the Apprehended Violence Order application and closed the door on them. She wasn't sure what was going to happen now. She just knew she had to see it through. It would all be over soon. Soon? Months, maybe years but it would be worth it in the end. She'd made her bed. Time to do some lying in it.

*****

Had she contributed to his desperate decision by denying him his religion? Nikki asked herself again the question to which the obvious answer was no. She hadn't denied him anything, merely said she wasn't the religious type. Well, was she? All her life she had argued convincingly against formal religions and their dogma. Even though she felt a strange, unexplainable jealousy at the faithfuls' ability to simply accept the concepts of God, Christ, etc, etc.

Maybe it was the teacher's inability to fully explain the concepts, answer her questions, but she just couldn't blindly accept what they said as, dare she say it, Gospel? Nikki had read the Old and the New Testaments, virtually word for word. She knew from her own study of history and anthropology that the Old Testament was mainly a rehash of numerous folk tales and myths from earlier tribal groups. As for the New Testament, written many years after the events and translated from Hebrew to Latin to English to whatever, the activities of Christian missionaries throughout history and their efforts to convert the heathen were enough to cast serious doubt in her mind.

She couldn't understand how intelligent people, fellow scientists and academics whose opinions she respected, could actually argue man had only been on this earth for 5000 years. Forget the historical and scientific proof to the contrary. Believe a collection of fairy stories instead. If that was the case, how come the Church never said boo whenever a member of the Aborigine community threw up the "my people have been on this land for forty thousand years" argument? One PC mob against another would fracture their attempt to have us all believe a load of twat so they probably had some tacit agreement not to rattle each others' cages. Typical. And that crap about Noah's sons and daughters-in-law bursting out of the Ark and populating the world all by themselves. They must have been busy because they had to create enough people to populate Egypt and supply a nation of Hebrew slaves for Moses to lead to freedom not a few hundred years later. Of course she knew it was never supposed to be historically or chronologically accurate, but why did these sky pilot's insist on spouting their drivel chapter and verse?

Still, she did envy their ability to have blind faith in those fairy stories. It must be such a comfort to be able to be selectively ignorant of any fact or detail that contradicts the dogma. Nikki shook her head again and resumed her construction of the perfect cup of coffee.

*****

Pete had endured the ride in the paddy wagon to the Police station, nothing inside the bare shell of the rear area to hang onto as the vehicle conveyed him into the due process of the law. He rolled awkwardly to the side as the vehicle fought the centrifugal effect of cornering, passing on its discomfort to those riding within. He was amused that there were no seat belts fitted. He wondered if any arrestee had ever sued the Police Service for damages as a result of an accident enroute to the lock up.

The vehicle stopped at a set of traffic lights in the middle of down town North Sydney. Pete looked around anxiously, just his luck someone he knew would be standing on the pavement, staring incredulously into the rear of the van at him. Then again, what did he have to be ashamed of? He had done nothing wrong, committed no crime. He was a victim of the surge in AVO's the state had recently experienced. Not his fault his wife was feeling vulnerable, guilty and ashamed. Pity he had to cop the consequences of her shame.

The van pulled into the garage of the station and the roller doors closed automatically behind him, shutting him off from the prying eyes of the world. As he was let out of the back, the thought hit him that he should have a jacket to throw over his head like the guys you see on the news. Well, there would be no camera's waiting here. Even if there were, Pete would stand tall and proud and look right down the barrel of the lens. The taller cop indicated he follow him towards the lifts and Pete did as he was bidden. For some strange reason he had a flash back to his military training in escape and evasion. What to do if captured as a POW.

That course had been two of the roughest weeks of his life. First up he had spent five days on the run in the bush wearing old clothes too big or too small, boots filled with leaves to help make them fit, no laces either. Cold, wet, hungry, it had almost been a relief to make it to the final checkpoint and be taken into captivity at last. Some guys hadn't made it that far, captured virtually right away and had spent the last three or four days cooped up in the back of a Land Rover.

Be the gray man, they had said. Don't play hero, don't resist, don't talk. Answer in yes and no style, don't offer a single word more than necessary to stay alive. Hold out as long as you could, but if you cracked, simply start again. Everybody cracked eventually but as most information on the battlefield was fairly time sensitive, the longer you held out the more worthless anything you had to say was. A bit different in a civilian context, but the principles were the same and Pete knew he could survive this. He very nearly hadn't survived the course.

Upon reaching the POW 'cage', which was actually the old gun emplacements at North Head, they had been shoved around and 'roughed' up by their captors. Then they had been interrogated for the first time, rough, brutal questioning. Then Pete had been left in a cell for some considerable time, maybe two or three days. Maybe only hours. The light had been left on, the cell floor was too short to stretch out on and the loud speaker had buzzed with white noise all the time. He was totally disoriented by the time they came for him again. No rough stuff this time. Virtually ignored him. No physical contact at all. After several days of this he was crying out for any kind of tactile stimulation, even a smack in the mouth. They had served bread and water for a few meals. Then breakfasts, three or four after each other, seemingly within hours. Then no food for a long time, then breakfasts again. Pete had counted to keep track of time and was served three breakfasts in 90 minutes. He ate the lot. Always liked breakfast and besides, he never knew when the next feed would come. Then they took away the slops bucket so he had to pee in the corner. They then fed him heavily salted food, but no water was supplied. Next up was the write your life story gig. Once you wrote it they questioned you, made you do it again. Then questioned you again on all the bits you added or left out. Clever bastards.

At the end of the 14 days, Pete had totally lost track of time and reality. He had forgotten it had only been an exercise, despite having clung to that one thought when all else in his world was turning upside down. His debriefing had been short, only two days with a couple of return visits a few months later to make sure he was ok. Some guys never fully recovered. Compared to that, this should be a piece of cake.

CHAPTER 7

Pete closed the door behind him and walked into the kitchen. He opened the fridge and grabbed the coke, the ice from the freezer and kicked both doors shut with his foot as he walked the load to the bench. He did the upper, fridge door as he laid the coke and ice down on the bench, leaning forward and doing a light, high back kick to shut the door. He used to practice high front kicks by switching on the lights but ended up taking a chunk out of one wall and Terri banned his daily 'martial arts-in-everyday-life' practice from then on. But she wasn't here to scold him for marking the fridge door with his shoes, now, was she? She was probably squirming under that scumbag of a rich bloke even as he thought about it.

Pete knew the futility of this train of thought, even though it was only natural. He kept having to erase images of his wife having sex with the ratbag. Some times he felt sickly turned on, at others just sick at the thought of his wife and another man. Stupid, really. She hadn't been a virgin when he met her yet the thought of her previous lovers never bothered him. Anything she did with scumbag she would have done before with her previous lovers. But she hadn't been his wife then, had she? And to Pete, that made all the difference in the world.

He made the bourbon and coke slightly stronger than he usually did. Not what you would call pub strength unless you were paying for a double. He took a long pull at the liquor and enjoyed the hit. Sitting down in his armchair he switched the remote on the stereo and took pot luck at what CD's were stacked within. Whitney Houston warbling her undying love for Kevin Costner filled the room with sound and memories. Terri had played the song continuously when she first got the album. As much as Pete liked the song, the singer and the movie, it had been too much of a good thing. Then they had both heard on the radio of a man in England divorcing his wife for playing that same song over and over and Terri had put the CD away for a few months. That was back when she loved him. A life time ago it seemed to Pete.

The random nature of life in the twenty first century played itself out in microcosm as the CD made its own mind up what it wanted to play next. Almost as if Terri had chosen this particular stereo for its latent ability to wound, Antonio Banderas started singing about his beautiful Maria of his soul, in Spanish. "The Mambo Kings" had been another movie they had shared together. Pete had loved the music and the romance of the story, Terri had loved the romance and the music. Seemed they had always liked similar things but for different reasons. The stereo went on choosing memories to hurt him by as he drank the contents of the bottle, mixed with the diminishing amounts of coke the situation seemed to call for. He figured he'd soon get to the stage where he would just set up an intravenous drip and lie back and let the booze do the job it had done for millions over the ages. Oblivion. Temporary detachment from reality with enough of a residual effect to make you feel you had paid your dues for the brief moments of freedom from pain and remorse.

Nine Inch Nails were copulating like wild beasts as he finished the first bottle. He hated that song. Terri had once played it whilst she danced for him. Only time he had seen her dance. She had danced on and on, teasing, tempting. It had gotten to be too much for Pete. He just wanted to slam her down and make her glad she was a woman. Terri had been in a trance, dancing to the music, Pete forgotten as she performed for an imaginary crowd of strange men, ogling her, wanting her, not being able to have her. Pete's insistence on consummating the mating ritual had shook her out of her reverie. Spoiling her mood. Making her hate him for not letting her dance on. She couldn't understand why he didn't get enough of a kick just watching. Why did he have to touch? She never let her audience touch her. And that was what Pete had become in her mind at that moment in time. Not her husband. Not her lover. Her audience. And audiences never touched.

Pete couldn't figure why she just kept on dancing. Okay, I'm hard already. Let's get stuck into it. He'd made a grab for her, playfully. She'd shrugged his hand away, not so playfully. A distant, almost hypnotic stare had malevolently bored into him. Through him. Yet it was as if she hadn't seen him. Didn't know it was Pete she had shrugged off. His ardour fell flat. Deflated. He'd stormed off into the bedroom, slamming the door behind him. Terri hadn't even missed a beat. He didn't know where she was but he did know she wasn't in their living room.

The CD chose another song at random, "Lover Come Back To Me" off a golden oldies album he had stacked in there. Pete fell asleep as some broad bemoaned the loss of her true love. Life went on, and on, and on. Just like a CD going round and round. Pete slept as the stereo continued to express its individual preference for music by mixing moods and melodies into a mélange of sound, tempo, rhythm and timbre. Pete's snores added a syncopated back beat as the stereo worked through the stack.

*****

There are places in society that deserve the title 'institution'. Marriage is a great institution, but who wants to live in an institution? goes the old joke. Looney bins are institutions. Schools, particularly those built after the first world war with their high windows and ceilings and hollow echoing corridors. Hospitals, even the new, modern ones where they try to make the patient feel a part of the healing process by talking about the 'management' of his or her particular illness. Gaols or jails. Police stations. Railway stations and government stores buildings. Institutions. But the taker of the cake for real institutional impact would have to be the court.

It doesn't matter whether it is an old court house that should be on the heritage list or one of the new microphone infested wood panelling jobs with subdued carpet, lighting and anything else the pinko architect could throw in to make the whole process more user friendly. Not that there was anything friendly when you were the accused.

Technically Pete wasn't accused of anything. He hadn't been charged with any offence. The police had conceded he had a right to attempt to see his wife and it was his word against the other blokes as to what went on. Conflicting statements, domestic drama, too bloody hard.

No, an AVO was simply an instrument of the court to ensure the protection of one person from another. Providing, of course, the restrained person had enough respect for the court and its jurisdiction, or fear of the consequences should they transgress. Otherwise it was simply a piece of paper and about as much use for the purposes of personal protection at the moment the offender decides to ignore its well chosen words as a zip pocket in a condom.

Pete was the subject of an Apprehended Violence Order. Or rather a temporary AVO in place until the court upheld or dismissed Terri's application for a full time AVO. It was not a criminal record kind of thing, not that that mattered to Pete. For him it was the principle of the matter. A matter of pride and justice. He was the injured party, not her. He was the cuckolded husband. That rich prat and his expensive legal advice could gloat all they liked that it was no longer a criminal offence to commit adultery in this state. But it was still wrong as far as Pete was concerned. Old fashioned? Maybe. But Pete had his principles. He would never have done it with another man's wife. Never had and never would although he had had his chances, before and after marrying Terri.

61

This particular courthouse was of the old variety. High ceilings and echoey corridors. Secret passageways leading from the cells below up to the court room, bars with spikes on top around the dock. Microphones needlessly added to rooms that were both acoustically and hermetically well designed. It was a warm day but the lazy beat of the ceiling fan provided sufficient downdraft to keep Pete's shirt from sticking to his back under his suit jacket. His mum fussed with his tie for the thousandth time until his dad gave her an AVO of his own. Then fixed the tie the right way once and for all. Pete suffered in silence, his defence to the imagined questions ringing nobly in his mind as he put the final touches to the much touched tie.

Pete found the listing amongst the others and passed on the court number and expected time of hearing. He knew he shouldn't but he went outside onto the verandah to catch a glimpse of Terri when she arrived. She would have to turn up or else the AVO would be dismissed. Not like the divorce hearing, whenever that would happen. Neither side had to be present, merely an administrative matter these days, divorces, according to the solicitor he had approached to get some advice on where he stood. A fee of five hundred dollars was lodged and then, providing the court was satisfied the separation had been in place for a year they declared divorce decree nisi followed a month later with decree absolut. That was it. No kids involved meant no custody wrangle, often a way to influence the property settlement.

Property settlement. The way Pete saw it she should get the clothes she ran off in and that's that. However, no blame divorce laws meant she would get fifty percent of everything that was accrued during their time together. Each would keep what they brought into the marriage and half of everything accrued since. All she had brought into the marriage was some clothes and her old car, long since gone. So she could have her current car and the payments, he would keep his. But Pete had entered the relationship with his own flat full of furniture and TV, video etc. Of course it had all since been thrown out and replaced with newer, more trendy stuff, but he had a right to ending up at least as well off as he started, surely? He was not going to be in his middle thirties and living in a flat sitting on bean bags and using a broom handle for a wardrobe rail to hang his clothes off. No way. He was used to a certain standard of living and he would keep it.

He was miles away, feeling self righteous when he saw her get out of a taxi and turn towards the court house. She paused as she saw him standing there at the top of the steps. Pete stepped back self consciously and Terri took that as a sign she could safely enter the court without fear of assault. Or whatever it was she was afraid of. Christ she looked stunning. And so vulnerable. Pete just wanted to take her in his arms and tell her everything would be alright. Idiot. She was taking him to court. She had him arrested for no reason. She had been screwing another guy, initially for money, for six months and he had been the stupid dope who knew nothing about it!

Pete still couldn't help feeling that way about her. He hadn't fallen out of love with her, remember. It had been her doing, all of this, this, this mess. Not his. He didn't even think it out of place he still felt that way about her and protective towards her. His parents watched her silently, yet he could see the anger they felt towards a woman they had, until recently, considered their own daughter. If it had been Pete who had done the dirty deed with another woman then they would have been here on her side. He was under no misconceptions about that. That same, simple, working class loyalty that held them all together during times of grief and crisis would have been turned well and truly against him if he had been the adulterer.

As they wandered back into the court house the female Police Prosecutor came over and introduced herself to Pete, mumbling something about there being no need for Pete to oppose the AVO as it wasn't a criminal charge and really all it meant was peace of mind for Terri as they both knew he wouldn't break it and so on and so forth. Pete looked at the woman and took a deep breath before he let her know exactly where he stood and that her little ploy might work nine times out of ten with poor, unsuspecting men worried about hurting their kids but it was not going to work with Pete. Furthermore, he would be mentioning this approach in the hearing.

*****

Debbie looked at the doctor in disbelief. OK, maybe not total disbelief but she was incredulous all the same. Of course she had known what the answer would be. What woman didn't know when she had a new life growing inside of her? She'd had two children before so she knew what it felt like. The signs and symptoms. Two months gone, huh? That would have been the time he did it with the slut, then came home and pretended he was so horny for her, when it was left over horn for the slut! Damn!

She was dressed and sitting down in his office, the thin ill-fitting robe she had worn during the examination back on its hook behind the door. She nodded at the appropriate times as the doctor went through his spiel.

The same one he gave to all his pregnant clients. He knew Debbie was going through a rough patch with John but he wasn't about to pry into the details of where the marriage was right this minute. Instead he added the bit he always gave the young girls. The bit about abortion and terminating and adopting out etc. He felt truly sorry for Debbie. 48 years old and going through a possible separation, maybe even a divorce. And now this. In all his years as a doctor he had never seen a single case of having a baby improving the marriage. So many couples thought that bringing another life into the world would answer all their problems and make them love one another again when the love had long gone. All it provided was a weapon to wound each other with in the cruelest war of all. And everyone, including the child, suffered.

Debbie heard the doctor and filed the words away for later absorption. Right now she was wrestling with her own feelings too much to pay any attention to anything else. How did she feel about this baby? Being John's baby made it good or bad? Would this bring him back home where he belonged? Is that what she really wanted? Debbie went through the saying goodbye ritual and left the office, auto pilot taking care of navigating the reception area, hallway, elevator and lobby until she bathed in sunshine and street noise. She needed a coffee, or maybe a drink. Yeah, a drink and maybe a few bucks through the slots. Give her time to think. She returned to her car and robotically headed for the club, her mind racing from salient point to salient point and never settling on anything remotely resembling a solution.

*****

Terri saw him on the verandah as she got out of the cab. He was looking at her and she felt like turning into slime and oozing her way down the drain. The cab had pulled in far enough from the kerb that she found herself still standing in the gutter as it drove off. How appropriate, she mused.

Summoning her courage and dignity she took a deep breath and stepped onto the pavement and marched to the court house entrance. All the while she felt Pete's eyes burning holes into her suit jacket and tight, yet not too short business skirt. She had chosen her clothes carefully. She wanted to be sexy and alluring to win over the magistrate, yet not appear trashy and slutty. She was, after all, the "mistress". The other woman in an affair. She needed to look vulnerable and in need of protection from a brute of a husband. One look across at Pete in his blazer and regimental tie and he looked more like a wounded puppy than someone in need of restraining.

She had been rehearsed by the Police Prosecutor and knew where to go, where to sit, what to do. She would have to say nothing unless Pete or his lawyer, if he had one, called upon her to answer questions. The female Police Prosecutor would do all the talking for her. She knew Pete couldn't afford a lawyer, but then he wouldn't need one. He knew his way around a court room and was articulate enough to defend himself. He'd done it before for that speeding charge and won. She wasn't sure if he would drag her over the coals, which was a possibility. But then maybe he would want to save her from that and also gain brownie points with the magistrate for being gentle on her. Who knew?

As she walked into the court room she saw his parents and sister and her husband sitting in a tight group at the back of the small room. She hadn't expected to see them and for a moment the emotions overwhelmed her. Pete's family had always been so good to her. They had been more of a family than her own immediate kin. Pete's sister was like the older sister she had never had, even acted as Matron of Honour at her wedding to Pete. She felt the tears flow from her eyes and she groped ineffectually for the handkerchief in her purse. The magistrate had already awarded her points for being so attractive, now his subconscious notched up a few more for her obvious vulnerability. This guy would have to be squeaky clean to get out of this one. And the magistrate didn't even know he had already made these decisions, such is the power of the sublime.

CHAPTER 8

Pete walked out of the court room feeling, well.....he wasn't a hundred percent sure how he felt. Vindicated? No. Free? No. The magistrate had virtually thrown the matter out, despite the best efforts of the female Police Prosecutor. She had really gone to town on him. Even had the gall to quietly suggest he accepted the AVO and didn't contest it. Just a formality she had said. Formality to her, maybe, but it was Pete's good name at stake here.

The beak had actually commented that he was under the impression that the prosecutor wanted everyone in the state to have an AVO out on someone. Make it easier all round if nobody could talk to anybody else. Pete had heard cops talking about the rise in applications for the restraining order. Most thought it was just a ploy to make it harder for the man to see his kids or get her more of a share in the property come settlement time. The limp dicked PC brigade would howl at that one but it certainly rang true with Pete. He knew a lot of guys who were on the receiving end of an AVO for no reason. It really made life difficult for them. They would have to spend a fortune getting legal help to get the Family Court to buy into the Local Court's AVO, something they were reluctant to do, obviously. Meanwhile she got free legal aid and some dyke generation-x-er with a hard-on against men who worked the system until the guy was either broke or broken. No justice there.

Pete said goodbye to his family and thanked them for their support. As he watched them walk off in their Sunday best he felt proud they were his parents and siblings. Simple, honest people. Never make a million bucks but the salt of the earth who would never let you down. They might not know much about Deeming or investments or share market fluctuations but they knew right from wrong and the meaning of the word staunch.

So what now, Pete old boy? Home to an empty house and a couple of hungry mutts or down the pub and drown a few sorrows? Pete never was a pub goer, so a few minutes later he found himself opening his front door and closing it gently behind him as he shut off the world. Hanging up his suit and getting changed into a pair of shorts, Pete went out to the garage and slipped on the bag mitts. As he worked up a sweat punching the bag his mind kept going back over everything that had happened in the last six months. He kept asking himself what he'd done wrong. What could he have done differently? Why?

*****

Nikki enjoyed the music and the singing. Or was it simply being amongst people who seemed to genuinely care? She had learnt to gloss over the technical details and not argue in her mind against every impossible fact the minister orated. Rather, she looked for the hidden meaning in the words. He spoke a lot of common sense and good values. A message she was ready to hear. She vaguely remembered something attributed to Nazi Reich's Minister Goebbels, something about if you tell a lie often enough even you will believe it as the truth. She recalled that missive less frequently now as she allowed herself to sink into the warmth of love and caring that enveloped the congregation at each service.

In the months following Don's death her life had changed immeasurably. She no longer hit the bottle. She took an interest in her friends, family, community. Everyone had been very kind. Her work was giving her solace and refuge whenever she had too much time on her hands to dwell on the twists of fate that had spiraled her into the now. Usually when the kids were with their father and his new wife for the weekend. She still couldn't bring herself to call that woman their step-mother. Too many connotations of childhood fairy tales where the word 'evil' always preceded the 'step'.

Nikki caught herself drifting off on a tangent and tried to pick up the thread of the sermon where her wandering thoughts had left off. The minister was speaking about faith. Strong, unwavering faith that everything was in good hands, the Lord's hands. A comforting thought for a single mother who was sick and tired of having to make decisions all of the time. Where to go, what to do, how to do it. Don had left the house half finished and she spent most of her free time playing painter, or carpenter or plumber. Good thing she had a university degree or two under her belt or she would never be able to decipher the instructions on the packs of glue, sealant, paint, you name it. She was on first name terms with the staff at the local hardware store. Knew which power tools did what and even lusted after her own work bench with integral vice and adjustable legs. Forget labour saving kitchen appliances, sanders, drills and grinders were her toys.

Nikki couldn't remember the last time she had been out to dinner with another human being over the age of twelve, let alone of the opposite sex. Grown-up things is what she missed, she realised. Grown-up girlie things like dates where the guy has it all planned. You just have to spend three hours and a small fortune to look like a million bucks and cover the reality with a little glitz and glam. He turns up, on time, you make him wait while he makes himself a little drink. Then off you go. He has reservations at the best restaurant in town, remembered to bring some flowers, dotes on your every word all night then…. Take him home and give him a little something on account. On account of if you don't he'll never call you again.

Nikki couldn't even bring herself to begin to think about getting back into the dating game. It was all too soon, too painful. Every word someone said, every song that wafted in from another room's radio. They all reminded her of Don. And Don's legacy was driving her nuts. Well, maybe not nuts but up the wall anyway. She was sick of Don. Sick of the reminders. Sick and thoroughly tired of having the memories. Why her? Why did her life have to take this path and give her all this, this, this… SHIT!

Nikki looked up and around at the congregation. Did she just say 'shit' out loud? It had been so loud in her mind, so real she was sure she had spoken the word and not just thought it. Everybody looked as if they were all in their own personal hells, long sermons had a tendency to do that to people, but then they might just be being polite. No, they were ignorant of her thoughts so she hadn't yelled out loud. Nikki chuckled inwardly at the whole scene and went back to trying to concentrate on the sermon. He was speaking about faith. Still.

*****

Debbie looked at John with contempt. The slimy, spineless slug had come crawling back to her, pleading, whining, begging. Well, maybe not as obviously as she made out but his intentions were clear. He wanted to make sure she didn't take him to the cleaners. Strip him of every penny he had, every scrap of furniture, personal possessions, you name it. She had news for him. And it was all bad. She would take him for everything and then come back for more when his superannuation was due. The growing life in her womb would help ensure her total victory.

"Sweetie, be reasonable. I have to be able to live too. I need my things, my suits, jewelry and basic furnishings. A TV, one of the videos, some paintings."

"Oh, sure, paintings are a necessity. Can't live without an original Pro Hart, can you?"

"Look, that was a present to me for my birthday. It's mine regardless." He tried to reason with her but he knew he was on a losing streak. She never had been one for logical argument, but what woman was?

"John" Debbie said drawing out the name into nine syllables as only an American could, " you can have your clothes and work materials, papers, laptop and so on. The furniture belongs to the house and is staying here. Like me. Where do you expect me to live? On the street?"

"I told you I would find you a nice apartment, closer to the city."

"I am not living in an apartment!" Actually the thought of not having a garden to worry about and being closer to some form of night life appealed to her, but she wasn't going to make this easy for him. " I am keeping this house and the Queensland house and the furniture. You are the one who did the dirty deed. You should suffer. Not me. Why should all I have be torn in half just because you got a hard-on?"

"The law says…" Debbie didn't let him finish recounting what his solicitor had explained to him in detail before he'd made his first move on the road to freeing himself of this shrew.

"I don't give a rat's ass what the law says. What is and isn't fair has nothing to do with the law of the land. It's the law of the jungle. You screwed me and cheated on me and have made my life a living hell. You deserve nothing. Nothing but shame and misery. I am about to have our baby and you still aren't man enough to fulfill your obligations to me. Your wife!" Debbie knew she was starting to lose the plot and rant and rave, but she couldn't help it. The anger was too much to bottle up any longer. She let it out of her soul in an explosive stream of hate and bitterness.

John gave up trying to calm her down, make her see reason. He was entitled to half of everything except the stuff she had brought into the marriage from her previous life. All he had brought was a few clothes, long since binned and some books. Everything he had was thanks to her. Pushing him to finish college. Supporting him by working at menial jobs so he could get his degree and then, it was her who made him go for the job at the company. Her confidence that pushed him to apply for a job he would never have had the guts to try for in the first place. He owed it all to her and he knew it. Not that that would stop him fighting her every inch of the way. The baby would be a problem, though. That could increase her share up to, maybe even over, seventy percent of everything.

As if reading his thoughts, Debbie renewed her diatribe. "This baby is not going to be brought up by a penniless single mother. I'm too old, John. I'm 48. I already have two grown up daughters. I've done my share of dirty diapers and 3am feeds. I will not do it alone again. You are the baby's father. It is your duty to be there for it. And for me, John. We both wanted this baby, you more than me. I knew what it would mean, you just think you'll have some cute photo's to show around the office, get a few pats on the back and come home after its been put to bed. You can play with it for a few minutes on weekends and then hand it back. Well that's not reality John. Babies are hard work. For the rest of their life, and ours." She took a breath and John took that as his cue to steal away.

"I have to go. Look, here's a cheque to cover your monthly expenses. I'll be in touch."

Debbie stood open mouthed as he simply turned and walked out of the room, down the hall and out of the house. The closing of the door punctuated her amazement and signalled her brain to resume talking. But there was no-one there to talk to. And there wouldn't be anyone to talk to for a long time. Debbie knew that. She'd been there before and she didn't want to go back. She'd known from the day she met John it would never last. What did he see in her? Back then he had been 19, young and innocent. She was 33, been there already and divorced with two teenage daughters but still very sexy to a guy like John. 'The Older Woman'. Not too old, just older enough to turn him on. It hadn't seemed to matter, the age thing. Not back then. But now. He was 34 and she was 48. Almost 50, damn it. Now there was a big difference. And that whore. What was she, 29, 30? How could she compete with that? Nature was cruel. Nature, time, tide, gravity. You name it and Debbie could blame it.

She heard John drive away and something in her snapped. She picked up a cushion and threw it at the Pro Hart on the wall. It missed. A bit like her life, really. Throwing harmless objects at stationary targets without a chance of doing any damage, even if she hit what she was aiming at. That last thought didn't really make a great deal of sense, but then nothing did nowadays.

*****

Pete got to the phone on the fifth ring. For some stupid reason he had this compulsion to pick it up within three or else he feared the caller would hang up. Stupid. Sure. But real in his mind nonetheless. He wasn't a compulsive/obsessive about it or anything requiring medical treatment.

No. Just one of those habit things. Like always putting his left shoe on first, then the right. Habit. We all have habits, some a little further out there then others, that's all.

It was Debbie, that bastard's wife. "Hi Debbie, how's it going?" he asked. He felt he was cheating on Terri just talking to the woman, which was just as stupid as his phone answering thing. He was doing nothing wrong. So why did he feel guilty?

"Hi, Pete. Listen, John was just here and he was trying to get some of his stuff. But I'm not going to make it easy for him. Hey, how would you like to help me get a little of our own back on him?"

Pete answered warily in the positive, wondering what she was about to suggest and if it would put him back in a cell. "What did you have in mind, Debbie?"

"Well, why don't we meet for a coffee and I'll tell you the plan. You are going to love it and it can't get either of us into any trouble. Trust me."

Pete wasn't sure about that, but he had nothing else to do so why not? "OK, I'll see you at the same place we met before in an hour." Debbie acknowledged and hung up, leaving Pete feeling a little uneasy about whatever it was she had in mind.

*****

"Damn her." John was going off the deep end and Terri had decided to let the 'boy' have his whinge, then she would smooth his ruffled feathers and make it all better. "She is going to fight me for every penny, even my own stuff. And there is a new development I hadn't mentioned before."

Terri sensed the next few minutes were not going to be her happiest to date, something about the way John had turned away from her as he spoke those last words. "What do you mean, John?" Terri asked, trying to sound as relaxed as she could.

"Debbie is pregnant."

The three words hit Terri like a jackhammer, whatever that was, she thought later. "PREGNANT!" Terri screamed out the word in an accusation that demanded to know why she had not been told this before and how long had he known and when was he going to tell her eventually and a thousand more questions crammed into one two syllable word.

71

"Pregnant!" she repeated. "If she is pregnant then you lose everything." *And so do I* her inner voice reminded her. "If she has a baby then not only does she get more in the settlement, but you will have to pay maintenance, the child will be your heir in precedence to any children that follow…" her words drifted off, not finishing but neither acknowledging that any future children would be borne by Terri. Something they had only discussed in the dreamy, slurpy way lovers do when they feel all gooey about each other after frantic sex.

John turned and started to explain to Terri why he had failed to mention this item so far, not wanting to worry her, not convinced Debbie wasn't just making it up to dig her claws in him, that sort of thing. Terri just let it go, knowing the real reason was he was basically a spineless bastard when it came to anything other than business where he was the Big Man in the company. How anyone could be so dynamic in the corporate world yet unable to wipe their arse in their personal life was beyond Terri. Which was why John was ideal for her. And her plans.

"Look" Terri tried to sound calm. "We can deny the baby is yours. Or we can wait and see and if it is born then get it checked for paternity. Personally, I think we have a good chance of not having to worry, after all, the old crone is 48 and late pregnancies are notoriously dangerous. For both mother and child." Terri looked at John as she finished her sentence and saw the dawn of realisation climb from the horizon of his eyes.

"You're right. She may not even make it full term. We'll just have to wait and see."

Terri spoke again. Obviously John was not quite on the same wavelength as she was. "John, it is up to you to make sure she doesn't go full term."

"What do you mean? Ask her to have an abortion?"

"I doubt she would agree, John. After all, this baby is going to be terrific leverage for her lawyer to turn the screws on you." Terri kept it short and sweet, hoping he would get the hint soon enough.

"So what do you mean? Surely you don't mean we force her to abort?" John was getting a little scared at where this conversation was heading. He knew Terri was tougher than she looked. He had given a very brief thought to inducing an abortion or miscarriage but had quickly dismissed the idea. That kind of intrigue was all very well in a Mills and Boon novel but this was real life.

"John, there are many ways that miscarriage can occur in a woman of her age. Anything from a fall down the stairs or in the bath to a scary ride in a car. The thing to remember is that you lose everything, and I mean everything, if that baby is born. The courts will have a field day with you."

John heard what she was saying but he wasn't taking it all in. He knew she was right, but he was not a murderer. And that was really what was being discussed here. The murder of an unborn child. His unborn child. John was and wasn't a lot of things, but this was over the edge. Terri, on the other hand, had nothing to lose. She had burned her bridges and jumped aboard his ship. If that ship was in danger of founding, then she would do everything to keep it afloat. Everything. And anything. John knew that. And it scared him more than the thought of losing his wealth. Much more.

*****

"So what do you think, Pete?" Debbie had finished explaining her plan and now sat back, watching Pete's face for any sign of disagreement.

"I like it. In fact, I love it." For the first time in quite a while, Pete was enjoying himself. Debbie's plan was not only above board and totally legal, more or less, it would hit that bastard right where he would hurt the most. More or less. "OK, so when do we do this thing?"

"Give me a call on my mobile tomorrow about lunch time. I'll have everything ready. Come round to the house, you have the address, right?" Pete nodded. "Good, then we will do it, bring the money and I will draw up the paperwork like my lawyer said."

"You are sure this is legit?" Pete asked again, although he had run through it in his mind and it made sense to him.

"Absolutely." There is nothing he can do, or the police or the courts. She may try and use it as leverage against you in your settlement but it won't count as she had left the matrimonial home before this so she has no say whatsoever in this. Trust me."

There was that phrase again, Pete mused. Nevertheless, she had come through each time so far and she really had more to lose than he did. So why not? Besides, it would be a great laugh. "What did he say about the baby?" Debbie had brought Pete up to date on that score.

"I think he realises how much the baby will decimate his share of everything. Personally, I don't want to bring a kid up at my age on my own. I have been thinking of getting an abortion, its still not too late."

"Might be best for both you and the baby." Pete said.

"Yes, but I don't want to lose the advantage the baby will give me in the settlement. Not because I want more. Hell, I'll get more than enough even without the baby. No, I just want to screw him over as much as I can."

Pete didn't feel comfortable with that sentiment. There was another, innocent human life involved here after all. He and Terri had always wanted a family. Stop that train of thought right there, Pete old son. "Well, watch your back because he might get a little desperate and try and do something, Debbie.

"John. No way. He's not the type. He doesn't have it in him. Trust me, I know him better than my own kids." Debbie returned to the bottom of her coffee cup and swilled down the dregs as Pete watched her over the rim of his own cup, raised as protection against his own thoughts escaping from his mind. Yeah, John wouldn't do that kind of thing. But maybe Terri might.

CHAPTER 9

Terri knew what it was she was after. The old, wizened Chinese man behind the counter looked at her over the rim of his spectacles and gave off the aura of having seen it all before. Everything. Everything man could do to man. Everything this planet could throw up at its inhabitants. Everything. Terri was sure he knew why she really wanted the Dit Ja Jow. Knew she wasn't pregnant. Knew it was for someone else. Just knew.

The old man, who was actually not that old but ten years running from the Americans and their B52's would make any ex-Viet Cong advisor look old before his time, knew the pretty woman in front of him wasn't pregnant. He also knew, although he would never acknowledge the fact, that she would never be pregnant. It was a gift. Or a curse. Depending on where you stood. His mother had been so blessed, and his grandmother. But not his sister. Funny how these things happen.

He had been sent to Vietnam to advise the Viet Cong on their insurgency campaign against the imperialist running dogs of the capitalist baby killers. He chuckled as even now the rhetoric he never believed himself then but espoused to all and sundry came tumbling back into his mind. He was from southern China, near the Vietnamese border and spoke the language like one of them. Yet he had never been the devoted party man they had thought he was. He had been taken prisoner just before the fall of Saigon, escaped by boat to this new land and now, a new life with a wife and family who knew nothing of his past.

The Chinese Medicine Store he had opened with the money he saved working every minute he had for five years was everything to him. He passionately believed in the herbal remedies and natural treatments he stocked and sold. He knew the strengths and the weaknesses of his potions. The ones that were used for good, and those that evil had manipulated for centuries. He looked into the eyes of the pretty young woman in front of him. He knew she was not pregnant like she had said. He knew she wanted to terminate 'a' pregnancy and that the Dit Ja Jow, normally used as a liniment for sore muscles and bruises, would terminate that pregnancy when taken orally. His curiosity was aroused by the fact that this western woman knew what all Chinese mid-wives had known for eons.

"So why not go and have abortion like everyone else? It legal here for you." He asked her.

"Yes, but I can't afford it and besides, this way is easier, right?"

"Oh, sure, just like miscarriage. Lots of blood and baby washed away. How long you pregnant?"

Terri was stumped. How long was Debbie into her pregnancy? More than a few weeks? More than a few months? She was chubby naturally, so she wasn't showing yet. So how far gone was she? It had to be relevant to how effective the potion was, surely?

"I'm not totally sure." She left it vague and reached for the bottle on the counter.

"You know, if the fetus is too far formed, then the miscarriage will be messy, as well as very dangerous. It could cause you to bleed to death if you not get treatment. You sure you want this?" The man was concerned. Not about the safety of some woman standing across his counter from him and obviously lying her head off. More because if someone died and it was traced back to him the press would have a field day. And maybe someone back home would see him on TV and recognise him, even after all these years. He knew this woman, who was probably buying the liniment for a friend, would not back down. He saw that in her eyes, too. So maybe she needed some real help?

"Look, I tell you what missy. Try this, it is like a ball of wax. You break it open and eat the thing inside. It is like a donut. This thins the blood the same as the liniment but it will cause the fetus to break up and dissolve. No danger like liniment of your friend dying." He realised he had acknowledged he knew it wasn't for her as she looked up and caught his eye quickly, before looking away and back to the strange object he held in front of him.

Terri smiled inwardly. Yes. This was what she had really been after but had forgotten what it was called. She had sat in on a seminar Pete had hosted for his martial arts students a few years back by a Chinese medicine expert. He had shown them how to make liniments for treating martial arts injuries and the side effects had been announced as part of the safety precautions. Funny what sticks in your mind over the years. This was the fool-proof abortion pill the Chinese had known about since before Jesus was a lad. She simply smiled at the man and asked how much. His reply showed he knew a captive audience when he played to one. $36.50 was far too much but still cheap at ten times the price for what she had in mind. Now, how to get the bitch to eat the damn thing. But she would leave that to John. He had to do something for once.

*****

John looked at Debbie, total disbelief in his eyes, shock etched across his face. He saw her mouth moving, making the same sounds he had heard her make only a few seconds ago but he refused to turn those sounds into intelligible words. Sounds like "sold the lot" and "all our paintings" and "those things we were going to give to the Salvo's" and so on. He simply refused to accept that she was telling him she had sold all of their furniture, paintings, joint property.

Debbie was happy. Happier than she had been for a long time. It had been worth it just to watch the expression on his face change from smug gloating, his usual demeanor, to the look of total, abject devastation he sported now. Bliss. Worth every second. But the best was yet to come. And he walked right into it with his next question.

"How much did you sell it all for?" He looked around and gestured vaguely with one hand, sweeping it expansively across the now empty hallway.

"One hundred big ones!" Debbie almost yelled it she was so happy. She had bet herself a million bucks he would ask how much before he asked who bought it. It was all working too well. Something had to go wrong, surely. No one could be this lucky.

"A hundred grand? It was worth that and half as much again." John couldn't believe his wife had sold all the paintings, investment pieces bought in lieu of savings or stocks for two thirds their value.

"Don't be silly honey. Not a hundred thousand. A hundred dollars." She was enjoying this far too much for it to be legal, surely? But her solicitor had been clear. She could sell her stuff and the joint property, but not his personal effects or anything she had given him as a gift. This was why the Pro Hart had remained on the wall. Pity, but you couldn't have everything even if she would have preferred to sell that over anything else. He so loved his Pro Hart.

John had sat down on the silly uncomfortable chair his wife had chosen to go with the silly, impractical telephone table in the hallway. "But John, it's a Louis the fourteenth." As if they had telephones in the 17th century. He could not accept his wife had sold their investment items for a hundred dollars. Surely there was a law against doing something like that? He reached for the telephone in a daze and dialed his lawyer via the stored speed dial numbers. Debbie was droning on as he listened to the phone ringing at the other end.

"Yeah, and guess what? Well, since it is joint property, either of us could dispose of it at will as we are both deemed by law to have equal interest in the property. The only stipulation, of course, is that I have to pay you half the money. Its not like we both have to agree to sell it because it is in the matrimonial home and either of us can decide what to do with it as we both own it 100% each as we are husband and wife. Since you left the matrimonial home you weren't available for consultation, which is more a moral issue than a legal requirement, so I decided to sell it all and we can share the money. This will make it so much easier to arrive at a decent property settlement before the divorce, don't you think?"

But John wasn't thinking of much right then other than the depressing news his lawyer was giving him via the telephone. She was right. There was nothing he could do about it right away unless she had gotten carried away and sold off something that it could be argued was his, in which case she would have to pay full compensation to the real value of the item. John knew in his heart of hearts that Debbie would not have made that mistake. No. She had planned this and she knew exactly what she had been doing. He mumbled something appropriate to the voice on the other end of the phone and hung up. Debbie was smiling at him with that silly look she reserved for idiot waiters and small children, a crisp fifty dollar bill in her outstretched hand.

"You will not get away with this." John tried to bluff her, knowing it was futile but something had to be done. A hundred and fifty grand worth of paintings. A large portion of his retirement assets that would have been worth ten times that when he pulled the plug at 55.

"I already have and there isn't a thing you can do about it." Debbie replied, dropping the money on the telephone table and walking away towards the kitchen. "Besides," she quipped over her shoulder, "don't you want to know who bought all the stuff?"

John leapt to his feet and followed her into the huge kitchen, keeping the island bench between himself and her throat, the like of which deserved an immediate throttling. "Who?" The single word came out louder than he had intended, but he had to know. Maybe he could sue them and get his goods back. Surely it was a crime to buy at such a bargain rate? Surely the Tax Office would want to know about this?

"Pete Graham. You know, 'slut's' husband." Debbie watched John closely, absorbing every nuance, images she would cherish for years to come etching themselves indelibly on her memory.

At first she was disappointed. It simply hadn't sunk in. Then it slowly began to dawn on John just who she meant. He looked at her. He raised a hand and pointed one finger at her. His lips shook as he tried to spit out the words his racing brain was forming into sentences, weighing up, discarding and re-configuring. All in a nano second. He went into overload and simply turned away, slumped against the island bench and dropped his head. He could not believe his wife had not only sold all of their paintings for a pittance. She had sold them to the man he had cuckolded. Any attempt to frighten the man into a deal via his lawyers would either smack of bullying or Graham would simply laugh at him. Well, not him. He wasn't going near the man. He meant his lawyer. No, the courts would not support him. What she had done was legal, if somewhat easily reversed by a good lawyer at settlement time. But the fact remained this time it would probably remain as is because of who she had sold the paintings too. Even to mention it at the property settlement would possibly jeopardize his chances of minimising his losses. He had been warned he would hurt, but not this much. And if she has the baby. Everything. He would lose everything.

Debbie could almost read his mind. It was as if he was thinking aloud. His pain was emblazoned for all the world to see. Well that serves him right. Bastard. There was nothing he could do. If he tried to pull anything with Pete he would get nowhere. If he tried to use this against her at the property settlement it would be objected to by her lawyer. He had advised her and knew what to expect. No, she was well within her rights according to the law. The same law that no longer sent him or the slut to jail for what they did. No longer gave her even grounds for divorce. What was happening to the world, and this state and its laws in particular? Who cares? The law was there to be manipulated to your own benefit. Always had been, always would be. And she could afford a great lawyer. She hadn't spent every penny of her inheritance. There was still a few thousand stashed away after her mother had passed on. Real money. US dollars. Yeah, she could afford a fight, and he was going to get one hell of a fight, that's for sure.

*****

Nikki knew he was watching her. She just knew in that way that women have. He was young, very young. What? Twenty five? Twenty six? He had been vaguely introduced in absentia by the hostess waving at his back and saying "that's Tim". He was cute, no doubt about that. Cute in that schoolboyish way some women find attractive. OK, she found it attractive too. She always had held a secret fantasy to be Mrs Robinson one day. Hell, she was nearly the wrong side of forty, the day had come.

Tim moved towards the bar, although it was hardly a real bar. The strongest drink on the trestle table was fruit juice or coffee, depending on whether you got the two hour old coffee or the month old left over from the Girl Guide fund raiser fruit juice. These church hall functions were often fraught with peril as far as the risk of food poisoning was concerned. Things were left in fridges that often spent days turned off after some well-meaning idiot switched off everything with the lights as they left the hall last.

Tim rarely came to these socials. He was shy, mixed up and pretty well inexperienced in life. At twenty five he had spent most of his life, twenty years of it in fact, in school. His parents died shortly after he started kindergarten at age five. Then his uncle became his guardian and promptly sent him off to boarding school. After boarding school there was university, which he was just free of, finally. Seven years to do his degree and then his Masters. He would do nothing for a year or two then go back for his Doctorate. Maybe take up a teaching post then.

He rarely thought of his parents, at least not consciously. The nightmares came less frequently since the therapy had started to do something for him. He wasn't sure what it was doing but he had to admit he felt a lot calmer, less likely to lose it over nothing like before. His uncle had been a major contributing factor to his psychosis, a very domineering male role model. Tim firmly believed a real man behaved exactly how his uncle behaved.

Nikki found herself pouring a glass of something vaguely resembling fruit juice at the exact same moment Tim was doing the same thing from the other side of the table. Her eyes raised themselves from the rim of the glass and glanced across at Tim as she stopped pouring and replaced the jug of juice on the table. Tim paused mid pour and did the same. There was something about him she could not deny she found exciting, attractive. Something she couldn't put her finger on, too, but it was there. It was just like when she first laid eyes on her husband, or Don. Something intangible, yet totally real. Dangerous. Volatile.

Tim managed to put down the jug of fruit juice before he spilt it all over the table. She was looking at him. Unashamedly. He almost blushed under her attention. He felt it too. Something about her. Christ, she was old enough to be his, well maybe not his mother but still. But she was a looker and so beautiful. And her age was almost like an added attraction. Hell, she was in great shape for twenty nine let alone thirty nine. He looked at the cleavage showing cheekily for a church function from the loose flowing hippy type kaftan she was draped in. He imagined she was not wearing a bra under there, could just about prove that from where he stood. Probably not wearing any knickers, either. He felt himself go hard and knew he was sinning. And here in the church hall and everything. It only made him want to sin some more. Then he could pray for absolution and be closer to his Lord. A surge of religious ardour rushed through his veins as he returned her hungry stare.

Nikki felt it begin deep in her loins. Her crotch was damp and aching with her need. It had been too long. She needed the youth and vitality this boy could offer her. She knew he would do as he was bidden. She put her glass down and looked again into his eyes. She licked her top lip slowly in preparation for opening the conversation and she knew the effect it had on him. That single, sensual action. He was hers for the taking.

Tim saw her pink tongue tip extend from between lush, un-coloured lips and wipe away the dryness of her top lip. In one, smooth motion she completed his erection and nearly took him over the top. He was hers. He knew it. He almost dropped the glass of fruit juice as he moved around the table to stand beside her and hear her speak for the first time.

"Hi" her voice almost cracked like a teenage boy's, changing from child to man. "My name's Nikki, you're Tim, right?" Tim nodded his reply and simply stood there, drinking her in and lapping her up like a puppy. A love sick puppy.

*****

Pete stacked the last of the paintings in the spare room. Spare now that Terri was gone and with her any chance of ever making this room the nursery. The chain of teddy bears stenciled around the walls mocked him and his memories of looming fatherhood. Terri's pregnancy had been the happiest time of his married life. She had glowed, really glowed. Just like the cliché only Terri had damn well glowed with health and happiness. Then the day when he came home to find the note taped to the door. A note hastily scribbled by his mate's wife, Pat. Terri's best friend it had turned out. They had done so much together, him and Blake, her and Pat. She loved their two little girls like they were her own. And now she was having one herself and Pat had been with her all along, going to doctor's appointments when Pete had to work. A true friend. And true to the end as she was right there when she was needed. Needed to rush Terri to the hospital as the baby they always wanted flushed itself from her womb in a miscarriage that had changed his beloved Terri for ever. Sent her off on this tangent that claimed their love and their lives.

Debbie was using him, he knew that. He didn't really care that the trick with the paintings was going to hurt John. That wouldn't bring his Terri back to him. It was a typically female thing, this getting back at him like this. Hitting him where it hurt instead of hitting him in public and cleansing the shame of her infidelity with the time-honoured smack in the mouth. He would hang on to these for a few months, just until the property settlement went through for Debbie and John. Then he would "sell" them back to her and get his hundred bucks back. He had declined any more out of principle. Could have, but wouldn't. No, he would be doing this as a favour to his ally in this war. Ally? Only because she wasn't an enemy. There were no winners or losers in this kind of warfare, just victims. Ally hardly seemed appropriate terminology for someone he probably wouldn't have liked under any other circumstances.

And what could she do if he decided not to re-sell the paintings to her? Nothing. She couldn't enter into anything like a legally binding re-purchase agreement with Pete without giving John's lawyers an opening to dissolve the sale to him and force him by subpoena to return the paintings and take back his money. So she was trusting him. Totally. At least to the value of a hundred and fifty grand. But she had something more to fall back on than any piece of paper. Any legally binding contract. Yeah, she wasn't stupid, this Debbie. She knew her man. She had Pete's word he would follow the plan. And that was worth more than any contract ever could be. At least it was to Pete. For what that was worth, which right now didn't look like much. But after all he had been through these past few months, it was all he had.

CHAPTER 10

Tim looked back at the rumpled sheets on his side of the bed as he headed off to the bathroom. "His" side of the bed was a little presumptuous, given he had been in the thing for less than an hour so far. It just felt right, though. It felt as if they had been together forever, or were destined to be. It felt right. Nikki wasn't like those college girls he had been with before. No, she was a woman and she made no bones about that or what she expected in bed. She told him what she wanted him to do. Demanded it. He liked that. Liked being told. Just as his mother would have done if she had lived. Told him what to do, that is, not sleep with him. Although it had crossed his mind. No harm in that, was there? An Oedipus complex was quite normal and healthy for a son. Maybe not when you were his age and had been an orphan since you were five, but still, lets not split hairs.

This must have been one of Tim's more lucid moments. Normally he was unaware of his feelings towards his mother, at least not consciously. Something in the passion Nikki had aroused in him must have balanced him out for a few, vital minutes. Enough so he could realise he did have unhealthy thoughts about his mother. Enough so he could make a mental note to bring it up at the next session with his therapist. Enough so he could realise once again how intense were his feelings for Nikki.

They had virtually ran from the church hall the first chance they had. He left and she followed almost immediately, any attempt at concealing their intentions from the rest of the congregation would have proven futile, such was their obvious haste. They hadn't even made it inside her car when she turned on his mouth like a hungry animal. Sucking, licking, enveloping his mouth with hers in a display of raw need. Tim was very perceptive, his kind often are. Despite their mental limitations, maybe because of them, they were very intuitive of a person's darker side. Their passions. Their desires. Tim had known what Nikki wanted all along. He had just known. And he knew how to give her what she craved.

*****

"No! For the last time Terri, no!" John almost stamped his foot like a spoilt child to emphasize his discontent at what she had just asked him to do. Ask? She had virtually ordered. No way. No way. He was not a murderer. She forgot the baby was his, or at least half his.

"If you don't do this then she will take you for all you are worth, and then some. Do you think we could live off what I could make? And would you want me working again?" She left the statement hang like some malevolent threat. She knew he would never let her return to the parlour. Those days were over and the pair of them were erasing all memory of the truth of how they met, where they met, why they met, from their collective minds. They were already telling friends and family they had met at the Marble Bar at the Hilton Hotel. They were even starting to believe it themselves.

"Terri, I couldn't do it even if I wanted to and I don't want to. How would I get her to eat the thing anyway? It's the size of a golf ball, it's not like I could slip it in her drink." The potion was, in fact shaped and sized similar to a golf ball, very dry looking and musty smelling. God alone knew what it tasted like.

"Think yourself lucky its not a suppository, John. How do you think you would slip that past her?" John ignored her wit and walked a pace or two away. As he turned she went on. "Look. You have to do something. We can not let that baby come on the scene and ruin everything. Right now it is just a blip on an ultrasound. Don't let it become anything more and it is not murder. " The logic sounded right to Terri, even though she would never have done such a thing had she ever become pregnant. No, she wanted her own baby far too much for that. Even more so after the...the....she could never bring herself to think the word, miscarriage. Her mind went blank. She knew what the word was and knew she was blanking it out. Couldn't help it. Probably for the best anyway.

"Terri, I will not assist my wife to abort our baby. Period. I would rather risk everything than have that on my conscience. Its alright for you, but I know it would haunt me and I don't want that kind of trauma in my life." John wasn't being noble, just, as usual, selfish. He didn't care about the foetus one bit. But he knew for some stupid reason he would feel awful if he helped abort it, so he refused because it would be better for him in the long run.

Classic coward symptoms, Terri thought as she looked at him My god. How can some men have all the character and no money whilst others have all the money and so little admirable character? John was ok on the surface, even seemed very admirable, likeable and a decent man.

But scratch the surface or pile on a little pressure and the real John surfaced. The selfish, whining John it was so easy to despise. Terri put the thought out of her head and refreshed herself with a mental image of John in a powerful pose, standing at his desk and about to sign the order to evict some tenant down on his commercial luck. Yes, that was the John she knew and, dare she say loved? Love? Who cares. It was too late now, her bed was made and it was time to do a little lying down. John could be a stepping stone to someone really wealthy. Really wealthy. Real money. Filthy rich.

*****

Why not? What did he have to lose? Let's face it, his marriage was over. Finished. Move on. Start a new life already. Still, he couldn't help feeling he was being unfaithful to Terri. Absurd? Yes, he knew it was absurd. But that's how he felt about it. Don't ask him to explain, he didn't understand why he felt that way. Hell, it was a major step forward that he actually recognised he did feel that way. At least with that feeling in the open he could deal with it better than if he kept it repressed.

So why not? He had to get back out there sooner or later. Hell, he needed to find himself someone. Someone not just to replace Terri but also to reaffirm his manhood, prove he was worth it and we all know the only measure of your value in society today once we get past houses, cars and job descriptions is whether you are a) married and b) is she a looker? Well Terri had really raised him up in the social stakes, even if he did lose a little with his job title and the address. And cars, well it was truly a matter of taste but Pete knew he lost out there. So it had all hinged on Terri and the fact that she was both beautiful and devoted to him.

Yeah, right. How would he hold his head in public now? Bad enough she left him but for another bloke. If he had at least slapped her around he was sure he'd win some grudging respect, despised sure, but respected all the same. But cuckolded.

Pete shook his head. He couldn't believe he had just thought that load of crap. Respect? Social stakes? What was he thinking of? He sat up in the chair and looked at the clock on the wall. Seven pee em, Saturday night. And was he going to spend another one sitting in front of the TV watching the same cop show? No. NO. He was getting himself shit, showered, shaved, shampooed and out.

He shook his head again at the recollection of his thought pattern. It made some sort of whacky sense, though. Many of his peers really did put enormous store in your address, job title and what you drove. They did value you by your mate, your life's partner. Those men with homely wives were pitied. Everyone knew they would get nowhere and still have to face the frump every morning. Those with super sexy wives might move up the ladder initially but as the wife started to screw around they would remain stagnant in their life and career until something gave. And those with attractive yet intelligent wives, well everyone knew they were destined for the top. The sky's the limit for them. You could tell. By the wives. True.

Pete figured he had been one of the latter, but developed into the middle kind. Strong initially but stagnant once 'the missus' did her thing. And his missus had done her thing, all right. Big time. He wondered if any of the blokes at the office had been her clients? Don't go there, Pete. Its all water under the bridge and nothing productive will come of it. Leave it well alone.

He went back to thinking how we do measure our success, and how we measure success in others, how they measure it in us. As he went about his ablutions in preparation for the "big night out", he thought how he had met married men with kids who, once they had spawned, became totally different people. It was as if they were lording it over those who hadn't been able to peg out the best rock and attract a full harem of females like some randy walrus. And the proof of his pudding was in her oven. Despite the fact the little mongrel looks like Winston Churchill living through diarrhea in miniature, everyone dutifully informs the parent/s how beautiful the child is. Despite the fact Dad was crapping on knowingly to the previous proud parent, now he had made the club he was oblivious to the wool falling swiftly over his face, denying his eyes the sight everyone else wished they couldn't see. Yet another ugly baby from a pair of ugly parents you wished nature had skimmed off the top of the gene pool long ago.

Crap Pete. Crap and you know it. You would have been just the same if your child had survived. Child? It had been a baby boy. He'd finally seen the ultra sound. Yeah, that far along they knew what it would have been had it lived. It? Him. It was a him and it was his him. His son. Pete leant against the bathroom doorway for support. He really had to stop doing this to himself. He was knocking himself out and for what? None of it would rewind his life of the past few months and bring things back to normal. Or what he had quietly enjoyed as normal.

For the next ten or twenty minutes he brushed away these conflicting thoughts that had been fighting for space in his head for a while now. Perfectly normal, his doctor had told him. Providing you realised you were doing it and snapped yourself back to reality. And if you didn't realise it? Pete had asked. "Then it goes on and on until you can no longer differentiate real from made up". Perhaps that is what happened to Terri? Perhaps this is why in a recent telephone conversation with him to sort out the property settlement she had told that load of cobblers?

Pete thought back just a day or so to the phone call. Terri had rung, late at night and sounded very depressed. Obviously 'he' wasn't there, otherwise she wouldn't be lonely and she wouldn't call. She had told him how Debbie had lied to John and told him she was pregnant. John knew this was a lie and told her. Debbie then went off her head and nearly killed John. And then she went on to say how it was like when she had lost her first child, forced to adopt him out shortly after birth. Adopt out? Pete had no recollection of ever hearing that story from Terri in all the years they had been married. Surely if she had given birth before they met and had the baby adopted out she would have made some mention of it?

Pete had even telephoned her mother who denied any knowledge of the birth but also implored Pete never to bother her with this kind of stuff again. After all, as she pointed out, he and Terri had their own lives to lead. In other words she cared so little for anyone other than herself she didn't want to know. And Terri's Dad was off interstate with a new wife, two new kids and the wonderful news he had written Terri out of his will because the "little ones" would need things more than her if he died before they were adults. The news had hit Terri so hard, proof finally her father didn't care for her. Still, it was par for the course and with dysfunctional parents like that, no wonder she had finally snapped.

Pete was dressed and putting on the last few drops of 'poof juice' so he would smell nice for the ladies. Still using Brut 33, it took him back to his Disco Days. Time to change the aftershave but it was all so damned expensive nowadays and who really cared? A drop behind each ear and he was off. Slamming the door closed behind him he hopped into his car and headed into town. Tonight was Singles Night at the RSL near Balmain. 28 plus the ad read. No jeans or casual attire, all men to wear ties. Ties? How archaic. As if a suit is going to guarantee a woman a decent man, just because he knows where to hire a suit. Pete had his own. A little tight, he had put on some weight since giving up the body guarding, but still wearable.

As he drove down the driveway and headed off into town he felt a growing sense of excitement. Maybe tonight he would meet the next Mrs Graham? Who knows? At least it would be a change from the television and take away Thai food.

*****

Terri was thinking hard. Thinking about the 'donut', as she had come to call the Chinese herbal remedy. John was next to useless. He wasn't plagued with any guilt about finishing off his unborn protégé. No, he was more scared about getting caught. Scared he would be found out by his peers, family. Her. He still adored the old slag, even though he lusted after Terri's harder, younger, more sensual body. She couldn't believe it, but that was the truth and she had better get used to it because for some reason, Terri felt that woman would haunt her for the rest of her days with John, however long that might be.

What if she had the baby? What would the consequences be for all concerned? Sure, John would lose more of his assets, but surely he would still keep a fair amount? He would have to pay a whopping amount of child support as it was done on a percentage of his income, not a base rate as it should be. Terri didn't think she might have thought differently if it had been her left alone with a baby. She wouldn't have cared. More than anything else in the world she wanted to be a mother. Which set off another train of thought.

What if Debbie had the baby and John got custody? It would be almost the same as having her own child, except without the stretch marks and saggy tits, not something she had been looking forward to, anyway. She would love it just as much as if it had been hers and Pe... She almost thought Pete's. John's. John's baby. Pete was history, past tense, gone, over with bar a few minor details of a legal nature. Mere tidying up, that's all that was left of that. Still, her first thought had been of Pete, she guessed that was natural after all those years of marriage. In fact, every day she thought of Pete less and less. Not to the stage where a day went by without her thinking of him, but getting there.

Hmmmm, the idea of her and John getting custody of the baby started to grow in her mind. How would they do it? Would the father have an equal chance at custody as the mother? Maybe. Maybe not. Those same 'no-blame' divorce laws might make it easier for her to have custody. Then again they might not. She needed an edge, some leverage to make sure she could get the baby. Already her mind flicked channels completely from the donut issue to the custody issue. A signpost to her mental state, her sudden about turn on the donut issue would surely throw John a curve ball but he was used to her about turns. At least this one went along the path he would prefer to choose.

Terri started to mull over the problem like a small dog worrying a large bone. She knew she just had to keep thinking about the issue at hand and the solution would present itself. Perhaps not all at once, but the key would appear and then other random thoughts would fall into place. It had all happened before. She might go and play her motivation tapes again. That was where she learnt to use the term issue or challenge instead of problem. It worked. Simple, but effective. Now, how would she save this baby from a life as a child to a single mother, and an ugly, old one at that. Terri giggled at her own joke and continued to think the puzzle through. The answers would come. It was just a matter of time. Meanwhile, perhaps she could use John's reluctance to serve Debbie the donut one more time. Set him up to embrace this new idea as if it was his own. Then he would fight tooth and nail for his child. See, it was working. Already ideas were coming to her.

*****

Tim pressed Nikki against the bed with the force of his thrusting. She was lying on her stomach, struggling for some reason to regain her balance and her dignity. Tim had a handful of her black hair in his right hand, pulling back on it in time to his thrusts like he was riding a horse. A wild horse. She was that horse and she thrust back as hard as she could.

His other hand cupped her breast, pinched her nipple and grabbed at her flesh. The pain was exquisite and shot through her in luscious waves of ecstasy. She tried to regain her hands and knees position and he again forced her almost flat on her stomach. She was writhing in frustrated pleasure, pinned down by his manliness. She felt submissive yet not subdued, as if her struggling kept her from giving in to him totally. She loved being under his control yet not conquered.

He thrust harder still, pulling her head savagely back with a tug on her hair that was anything but loving. She felt her neck ripped back and her back arched in response. This caused him to deepen his penetration of her automatically. She gasped at the heady mixture of pain and excitement. She managed to get one elbow propped under her and reached up with the other hand to grab hold of the bed head. Supporting herself in this way she was able to regain her hands and knees stance all the while taking every thrust and giving one back of her own.

Better balanced she really began to go blow for blow with him. With each punch of his member into her loins she rallied with a thrust of her own. Together the two of them increased their tempo and power until the room shook with their passion. Breath coming in spurts and gasps they rammed their bodies into each other again and again. With a Herculean effort Tim forced her flat on her stomach again and reached around with his breast hand to her mouth. He offered her his fingers and thumb and she sucked them in greedily, proxy for his manhood.

Pumping harder and harder until finally the earth truly did move for both of them, they simultaneously exploded together in an orgasmic concerto rare amongst anyone other than the pretend lovers of a porno flick. No faking here, both people, man and woman, arriving at a climax at exactly the same moment. Both lay exhausted, sated and completely in awe of what they had just shared.

Yet share was not the word one of them would have used if asked to describe their mutual peak. One of them had thoughts only for their own gratification. That the other had responded so hungrily, so uniformly, so synchronistically was immaterial for one of them. For that one had time and feelings for only one person in the entire world. Themselves. No one else mattered. Anyone else was merely a tool to be used to build the world their way. For them. Other people were irrelevant, of no consequence unless they directly or indirectly aided and abetted the obtaining of what was needed for ones success. Or stood in ones path.

*****

Nikki looked at Tim, sprawled half across the bed, eyes closed, breathing hard. She felt unbelievable. Bad English she knew but that was how she felt. Or was in unbelievably great? Who cared? She had just had the best sex she had ever had in her entire life. And what defined great sex? An orgasm was an orgasm. Sure, some were better than others, lasted longer, had taken longer to get there and given far more value for money than others. But what made this the best ever? Lack of memory of better times? No. It was Tim. Tim did it. The way he made love as if... Hell. It wasn't love making. It was sex. Fucking. Simple as that. No way did he make love.

Nikki knew Tim didn't care who it was he was screwing, not really. She knew that. She wasn't stupid. She'd sensed that pretty much straight away, at least the second time they had screwed, anyway. His youth and vitality meant he just kept coming back for more. Didn't last as long as Don had. Older guys tend to last longer but do it less often, take longer to get going and get back, so to speak. Not Tim. He was rock hard right away and then, as soon as he was spent he was virtually ready again. Suited her. Nice for a change, anyway. Kind of made her feel it was her who did it to him. She knew that wasn't the real reason, or all of the reason. But it didn't hurt to pretend.

She knew it wouldn't last, either. Just knew. Never mind. Who cared how long it lasted just so long as it didn't end right this very minute. No, give him a few minutes to relax and then start working on him again. As she looked up from the object of her attention Tim opened his eyes and smiled. He was thinking the same thing, the randy bugger, Nikki thought. Actually, he wasn't thinking the same thing at all.

CHAPTER 11

"Fifteen dollars, please. That includes a supper about nine." The lady at the desk just outside the door was mid forties, well dressed, even elegant as per the ad, (Singles Dance, 28 Plus - Gentlemen Collar and Tie, Ladies Elegant, Light Supper) one could say. She had a reinforced hair-do that would hold off the worst of several Atlantic storms should she ever find herself employed as a lighthouse off the Newfoundland coast. Pete handed her the money and wondered absentmindedly about the supper. Probably a piece of chicken and a couple of veggies, typical wedding reception fare.

The large room, or auditorium, where the dance was being held looked like it had probably seen a wedding or two. Along with a variety of tawdry political rallies, some ethnic performers of little note amongst their kin from the mother country and the odd disco. The obligatory mirror ball revolved around its glittering axis sending sparkles of light out in all directions to dazzle, confuse and set the mood. But what mood was it really setting and what mood was Pete in?

Not a particularly positive one as he scanned the early arrivals. Like most dances he had attended throughout his 'going out' life, the early attendees were the ones eager to change their lives by meeting him or her and figured they might miss them if they got there too late, like seven thirty or eight. The reality was that the winners in this game rocked up pissed after ten, paid nothing, wandered in, captured the best looking chicks and sauntered out for a night of guaranteed sex. All the nice guys could do was stand idly by and watch as the woman they had been mentally chatting up for hours as their courage levels rose was whisked away in front of their very noses.

There was a definite lesson to be learnt there and Pete had actually learnt it. Get in, get out and don't take no for an answer. By that he didn't mean rape the poor girl. No, he meant that this was a numbers game. You wouldn't meet 'HER', here. She was not that kind of woman. You came here in truth to get laid. So did everyone else, male and female. So, providing you didn't con yourself with more nobler ideals, the pattern was fairly simple. Scope out the possibles, target them in order of good looks up first and then away you go. Hit the first one and give her some chat.

Put the bite on her and if she isn't taking the bait, move on. Maximum investment of time, 20 minutes. Dollars? Two drinks, tops. This is the best looking chick in the place, remember. You might score in which case it is an early away to a better venue or straight into the sack. If you crash, who cares? At least everyone witnessing your public humiliation realises you were shot down by the best chick there. That earns a grudging respect from male and female, alike.

So the next one you hit knows she is second on your list. So what? You are probably not telling her anything new, here. She should have the same amount of time, afterall the night is still young, but now you are on a one drink limit. You need to stay sober enough to drive and perform, yet gradually get to the stage where you can do it with your last choice if it comes to that, heaven forbid it does.

Getting laid is a contact sport, a numbers game. Nothing more and nothing less. Once this strategic fact is grasped and applied, your whole life changes for the better. You will score more often, and more often with number one or two than miss bush pig down the end of the list. And don't get all noble about your attitude to her based on her looks. She knows she isn't up there with the best of the best. Again, this is not something she hasn't figured out for herself. You don't care about the numerous good qualities she possesses because you are simply trying to find another human of the opposite sex to screw. That's it so don't get all gooey on me. Pete had realised it was not his mission in life to iron out the inequalities of this world. Ugly girls got their share, many guys preferring them as they felt they would be grateful for the attention and not screw around. Well, Pete didn't know how much truth was in that rumour seeing as how inside they were made of the same stuff as the stunners who did play up, but it seemed to work. It wasn't Pete's job to make sure every ugly person ended up with a partner to mate with. Nature did that. Afterall, you were looking at the result of one of her unions right in front of you. She got made, so her mum must have got laid. And she was no oil painting either, judging by her daughter. Same goes for the sons.

By the time Pete had worked this all through in his mind he had equipped himself with a liquid shield to hide behind whilst he surveyed the talent in the room, checked out potential rivals and found out where the exits and toilets were. Toilets being particularly important as every woman at some time would pass through the portals of the powder room, a good way to make sure you missed no-one without having to wander around like the lost tribe of Israel. It had been nearly a decade since he was last on the battlefield but the old combat survival skills were rushing back to him. Honed over years of being single, often without the backup of others of his ilk as the casualty rate rose thanks to their ultimate success. You won the battles, they won the war. You thought you were winning if you did the deed, she knew it was more a war of attrition and she could outlast you any day. Talk about a Pyrrhic victory. If you really got lucky and struck pay dirt with a stunner, your defences were chemically dissolved by the love bug and you became a POW by choice. She then held the cards as your life changed for ever. No longer the carefree single guy, you were now a married man, marked for life and that was that.

Pete knew all of this but it had been many years since he had been in action. Back then he was at the height of his career when he fell for Terri. He was the best of the best, no beginner's luck for him. Now he felt like he was starting all over again and he was. That brought with it the burden of guilt. He still felt he had to be polite, nice to each and every woman and not hurt anyone's feelings. Pretend any of this actually meant something. And that would prove the downfall of any man out to get his end away. You could never confuse finding 'HER' with getting laid and all those who did never succeeded at either task.

Pete had given himself the verbal once over in the car coming here but he knew it was hopeless. It was still too soon and he couldn't just click back into hunter-killer mode. Nope, tonight he would look around, get the feel for the scene and maybe talk to someone, even have a dance. But he knew he wouldn't be getting laid. He just knew.

*****

"So let me see if I hear you correctly, Terri?" John reiterated. "You think Debbie is going to use the baby to clean me out of everything. This makes her mentally unbalanced and therefore unsuitable as a mother, so I should fight for custody and therefore protect the baby from her whilst at the same time keeping most of my assets. Is this about right?"

Terri simply nodded, glad the man was finally hearing what she had just spent two hours telling him.

"So no need for her to eat the donut and abort the baby?" John was openly relieved about this. He had no stomach for what was, in reality, murder. Even if it was murder of something not fully living just yet.

"Yes. Look John, I thought so hard about how you felt about the donut it finally dawned on me how much you really want to be a father. Otherwise how would you explain such noble, protective instincts?" She watched John's face as he digested this and imperceptibly nodded his agreement.

"So when you get right down to it, I am right. She is using this baby to get at you and that is not fair, especially given how you feel about the baby. She doesn't deserve to take away all you have worked so hard for. You know we talked about our baby and well, I guess it is simply bringing our plans forward a little. The big benefit is the baby will be better looked after with you giving it proper fatherly input instead of the one or two days a fortnight you would be lucky to get with her in charge. And yes, I do think she must be looney to try to hurt you this way. Of course proving it will be the difficult thing. So our main argument must be how much better off the baby will be in your custody. That you can give it so much more than she can will be obvious. We'll let her have access, generous access. At first. Then we'll quietly push her out of the picture." She let the last word hang, knowing John would pick up on it in his confident, 'now I have the answer I can stop whining' mode.

"Exactly." He thought how having a family and a stunning young wife would complete the picture of the successful young executive well on his way to the very top. Head hunters everywhere would be looking to poach him at seven figure salaries. Maybe he was overreacting to being let off the donut hook, but he was relieved. He seized this new development because it also gave him so much more than just the escape from being an accessory to murder. It would give him the perfect family. He could work his heart out, after all that was what really gave him satisfaction. He had the 'little woman' to come home to after nine each night. On weekends when he wasn't working they could enjoy the café society lifestyle and be seen in all the best places. Of course he would always spend Saturday morning in the office, carefully casual in designer jeans, shirt and loafers worth a grand all up but indicative to all that he was "in mufti". Maybe even the odd Sunday just to show upstairs how totally dedicated he really was? Accidentally run into the boss at the copier as he did his own admin work and mumble something about just dropping in to finish off that report or whatever?

"Yes." He said. "I think you are right, dear Terri. But how do we convince Debbie to let me have custody?"

"We don't." Terri replied, amazed at how dense such a smart, powerful man could be on some subjects. "We only have to convince a court."

John thought that might be harder than convincing Debbie but on further reflection he realised Terri was right. A court of law was a pushover compared to his wife. Ex-wife, or soon to be ex, that is. Yes, let her have the baby. Play the concerned expectant father all along and then, once the baby was here and happening, hit her for custody. He'd have a word with his lawyer tomorrow.

Terri turned away, satisfied she had put into train events that would give her exactly what she wanted. Everything she wanted. The man, the house, the baby, everything. It would be perfect. She saw their house in her mind's eye. She was standing at the front door with the baby on her hip as she kissed the man goodbye. She visualised his back turning away and heading toward the car parked in the driveway. The shape of his back was not the same as Johns, that she was certain, No, it was bigger, broader, more like.......She shook her head and cleared the vision from her mind. She turned around and looked at John. His mind was working away at a hundred miles an hour, she could see that. He was waffling on about the office, the baby, all sorts of things. For some reason, right then and there, Terri felt it was all unreal. As if it wasn't happening. Or going to happen. And she couldn't explain to herself why she felt that way. She just did.

*****

Debbie sat down in the only available chair in the waiting room. Aptly named, waiting rooms. She had waited in a few of them in her lifetime. First as a child with her mother, later with her unborn child as she became a mother for the first time. Or was that just 'became a mother'?. Surely once a mother you remain a mother forever, even if the baby later dies? Or you have one or more additional children? How can you become a mother for a second or third time whilst still a mother with the first one?

She was snapped out of her train of thought by the departure of one swollen belly and the shuffling to the door of another. The doctor held the door open for the next contributor to his weekend holiday home fund and noticed Debbie sitting near the magazine pile. He gave the wordless smile and raised eyebrow signal approved for use by doctors around the world in just such an occasion. Debbie smiled back, knowing she was not permitted to infringe on the other ladies' time with the doctor by actually saying hello just yet. The doctor quickly ushered the woman into his office and shut the door on any attempt by Debbie to bypass the protocol.

Instead, she reached for a magazine and started to ruffle through it, now and again licking a finger to help turn the pages. Typical women's magazine trivia flowed in and out of her consciousness as she let her mind drift to other things. She was, after all, worried.

Worried about the baby. She was getting on in life to be breeding. She was 48 next birthday if she was honest with herself, 43 if she wasn't. By the time the baby was old enough to vote she would be 66. Sixty six for Christ's sake! She would be a candidate for a retirement village and her baby wasn't even drinking legally. As the kid hit High School she was eligible for an old age pension. Her oldest daughter already had a ten year old son. She started to do the math in her head about the other grandkids from her two children of her first marriage and gave up as she realised the youngest would still be older than their aunt or uncle. She'd end up in the damn women's magazine herself as a cover story!

Debbie tossed the magazine away virtually unread yet absent mindedly reached for another one as she thought on. What were her chances of finding love again as a middle aged single mum? Single mum? That sounded so welfare. Sole parent, please. So what were her chances some fifty something guy, well established and free from any hindrances would want to get involved with a woman her age still picking kids up at day care. Unable to drop everything for a romantic week away in the tropics because junior needed to get to football training or ballet and school holidays meant entertaining the child and its friends all day with no respite. Hell no. She had already done that once. That had been bad enough, but she knew in her heart of hearts she couldn't face it again. Not alone. Not at her age.

She was here today to explore her alternatives. It would have been fine if she was still with John. No question as to what they would do. But there is a world of difference bringing up a child in a stable, loving family atmosphere and coping with the hardships of doing it all on your own. It was too much to even contemplate. So what were her alternatives? That was why she was here today. At least find out the viability of one or two of them. Get a professional opinion as to whether she could have an abortion, adopt the baby out, or whatever. She only knew one thing for certain. There was no way she could face having this baby alone. Unlike teenage girls who think it will be wonderful to have a baby of your very own to cuddle and be the center of attention with, Debbie knew two things teenage mums rarely knew. Babies are hard work and they are for keeps. You can't hand them back, you rarely get a break and the novelty wears off real quick.

The doctor was at the door again, farewelling one stomach and hailing another. He did the nod and smile at the lady who had arrived since his last emergence into the light of day and Debbie knew she was next but one. Time for another magazine.

*****

Tim was a natural with the kids, Nikki thought. She watched them playing together over her coffee cup, a stupid grin forcing itself onto her face despite her best efforts to control her emotions. Of course it was important the children like whoever she brought into their lives as a partner for herself. She didn't think of Tim as a father for them. They still had their father and there wasn't much she could do about that, even if she wanted to.

Tim swung her daughter around in a circle and they both fell onto the sofa, laughing and panting for breath. Tim was closer in age to her son than he was to her, it seemed at that moment as she watched them all playing together. The math didn't agree with her thoughts but other observers would have concurred with the sentiment. Still, what has age got to do with anything? Calendar years mean nothing, surely? What about that book she had read years ago, about the old woman and the young boy getting it on? "Harold and Maude" That was it. That had addressed a number of these issues, even been made into a movie. She remembered how warm the book had left her feeling. If only real life was like that.

Tim had instructed the kids to run outside screaming and yelling, at least it seemed that way as they departed the living room for the wrap-around verandah. The young man who had entrenched himself so deeply and so rapidly into her life closed the distance between them in a step or two and stood, still breathing hard from the play, looking into her eyes. Nikki felt herself waver under his scrutiny. Almost as if he was hypnotizing her, she thought. If he was then his spell was working. She felt in love, loved and very much alive now Tim was in her life. It had only been, what, hell. It had been just three weeks since they met at the church dance and this weekend Tim moved his things into her house.

Still, it felt right. Just watching him and the kids echoed that feeling. Tim drew Nikki to him as he leaned over her and kissed her hard and passionately on the mouth. Despite the awkward angle her half sitting, half standing posture leant to her she made no attempt to move into a more comfortable position lest it cause this delicious kiss to stop. And after all the hurt Nikki had been through she never wanted to feel that kind of pain again. Gravity took over and she fell back onto the chair, Tim being drawn down with her, still firmly attached at the lips.

Outside the children squealed and yelled, oblivious to the rising emotions being fostered inside the family home. Nikki wanted Tim so badly she almost forgot they were out there. Tim pressed her back into the seat with his lips so she was momentarily safe from rushing him off to the bedroom or the bathroom or anywhere there was a lock on the door and some slight protection from discovery or interruption. Interruption it would be for there was nothing to discover about her and Tim. The whole world could see she was as in love with him as he was with her. This was it. This was the real thing. This was how it was meant to be, how it should have been before and how it would always be from now on. Nikki knew that. She just knew.

*****

Pete loved this song. He just had to dance to it, simple as that. He put his drink down on the table and stood up. She had noticed him watching her, he was sure of that. So what? Let them know you are interested, have seen the bait so to speak. He walked straight up to her and asked her to dance.

For some reason, perhaps it was good manners finally catching up through the harsh reality of advancing age, but all the women here never refused a polite request to dance. Just as his mother had told him when he was 12 and off to the school social. It had been the case then because the girls had been told by their mothers not to refuse a polite invitation. They knew the risk of being left on the shelf. Then there was the reality gap of twenty or so years when blokes would get knocked back regularly whilst the women lived on the razors edge of fading beauty. Now, with the jolt of separation shaking some sense into them these women had remembered what mum had instilled in them so many years ago and they always accepted a polite invitation to dance.

Pete was glad of that as he led her onto the floor and began gyrating to the music. She had an annoying way of running her hands over her head like she was smoothing down a cowl or something. This was obviously her favourite dance movement and probably looked cool back in the 70's but did nothing for her now. Pete put her age at, well, how old was she? He was out of practice at guessing ages and she was not as young looking as Terri who was five years his junior and looked five more. No, this woman was the same age as him it turned out when he asked her. He had made the comment how he was sure she was younger than that going by her looks and she swallowed the lie like a pro.

The song ended and Pete was ready to sit down again but she wanted to keep on dancing. Fine, Pete could do with the exercise. They talked as best they could over the noise of the music. Pete was handicapped by not being able to hear what she said via his hand on her arse. He had seen a few guys here who, it seemed, could only hear what their partners said in reply to their asinine questions if they made physical contact with them. Usually with a hand on their butt. Oh, it started off hovering an inch or so off the shoulder blade. Then it actually made contact with the shoulder blade and then, with each question getting more and more in-depth, the listening hand needed to travel down to their arse where it could hear the answer so much better. Made him sick to see such blatant feeling up but he had to hand it to these guys, it seemed to work. Were these women really oblivious to what these guys were doing? Or did they like it? Or maybe they didn't want to cause a scene and would suffer in silence before dumping the guy as soon as they could break free. Who knew?

At last Pete steered her away from the floor and back to her seat where she invited him to join her. This was looking up. Pete sorted out the drinks whilst she visited the ladies to freshen herself up and it appeared the night had taken a positive turn. Pete returned to the table only to watch his possible score being professionally intercepted by one of the afore said bum listeners. Smoothly the lounge lizard wafted her onto the dance floor and began his mating ritual. She seemed to have forgotten Pete was back at her table looking after her G and T. Well, Pete could either move on and ignore this treachery, or fight back. Not that she was worth fighting for, all things considered. She was no Terri, this woman.

CHAPTER 12

The doctor looked at Debbie and evaluated the woman who sat before him. Forty eight years old, good health, average looks, shrewd brain. An interesting package, one could say. As a doctor he had to look at all the angles, not just the physical health of his patients. Mental stability, job prospects, home drama's, you name it, he took it into consideration if he was aware of it. In his forty years of practicing medicine he had come to realise that not everything was attributable to just one symptom, nor was it fixed by one simple pill. Patients, by that of course he meant people, were as different as the ailments they presented with. Like an iceberg, most of what was bothering them was beneath the surface, invisible to the eye.

"So, I need to know where I stand Paul. What are my options? I'm too old to go through this pregnancy without John." Debbie had been frank with Paul Gleeson, M.D., she always had been, ever since he brought her daughters into the world a quarter of a century ago, or near enough.

"Debbie, I'm sorry John did what he did. He has a lot to answer for, to you and to his conscience. But I am concerned with what we are going to do for you in the here and now. You are too far gone at your age for an abortion. At least any abortion I would sanction. Get a second opinion if you must but it will be risky given your history and what happened with your youngest." Both of them remembered the trouble she had experienced with her last pregnancy. Only swift action by Gleeson and his team had saved mother and child. Debbie did not want to have to spend the next five months worrying about a repeat performance on that scale.

"So what will happen if I go full term?"

"It will be a caesarian, of course, more than likely anything up to six weeks premature and therefore starting off behind the eight ball. Your emotional condition between now and then will play a big part on the end result, you know that. I'm glad you gave up the fags and the booze. I know it will be tough, especially going through this separation with John, but it is for the best. Your health and the baby's!" Gleeson finished off with the 'look'. Debbie had seen it before and knew it simply meant the man cared. Genuinely cared for her welfare and her unborn child's.

"I can't bring the kid up by myself, not at my age Paul. I'm a grandmother for Christ's sake, not a single mother." A note of desperation tinged with sarcasm inflected her sentence with a haunting timbre Paul Gleeson couldn't have failed to pick up on even if he was stone deaf.

"Debbie, I don't have the one, simple 'right' answer. I'm a physician, not a fortune teller. Go home, give it some thought, call this number and talk to the counselors. Think it through and the answer will come. Trust me, it will come. Meanwhile it is important, no imperative, you stay healthy and as happy as the circumstances allow. Your mood is your choice. Don't waste a moment being bitter, Debbie. It won't change a thing." He placed his hand on the back of her chair as he stood over her, silently signaling her time was over and he had done all he could. The rest was up to her.

She stood. Mumbled her thanks and farewells. Walked to the door and beat him to the handle, opening it for herself and stepping out in one fluid movement. He said goodbye again then automatically gave his hello signal to the latest patient in the waiting room. Debbie walked out and past the reception desk pausing only long enough to take the slip with her next appointment scribbled on it.

Outside the practise she walked along the hallway towards the lift. Exiting the lift she left the building and was bathed in sunshine however it neither registered nor changed her mood in the slightest. She was deep in thought and miles away as she stepped onto the main road, her auto-pilot taking her back to her car parked across the road and a few hundred yards further up.

By some stroke of luck or a convention of guardian angels exercising their rights to perform miracles, Debbie made it across the road without a single car coming in contact with her earthly frame. Her mind was on another plane, coming to terms with the reality of single motherhood at such an advanced age. Even falling pregnant had been a miracle, surely. What ever happened to menopause? Wasn't that supposed to have swept in and sorted out her periods, facial hair and mood swings in one fell swoop?

By the time she sat in the driver's seat and used the ignition key to parole some background music from its cell on the dashboard her mind had returned to her body and she let her shoulders slump. She rested her head on the steering wheel and sobbed. She cried because she did not want to have this baby without the man she loved. Yes, loved. Despite all he had done she loved him. Was it some kind of Oedipus complex where she felt more of a motherly love for him, therefore forgiving his trespass with another woman as all mothers must do of their sons? Was it simply the fact she was the age she was therefore vulnerable? Worried she would never find love again? Did having a younger lover vindicate her? Make her more attractive to other men? Build her self esteem?

Debbie had not thought about her and John for many years. Oh, she had thought about him but not in any way analyzing their relationship. She knew people stared when they were first introduced. More now than ever before. But John had always looked older than his years, mainly because she had dressed him that way. All the better to get the top job at such an early age. People didn't take youth seriously enough, despite the person's unquestioned ability to perform. Appearances, it was all about appearances. And hers had aged much faster, lately. Whilst he stayed majestically static she had visibly gotten older. He had even mentioned it. Tried to be nice, even funny. But still noticed. As if she hadn't noticed the same thing only years earlier?

And now her body was telling her she could have this last child, this last gift from John. Then what? Turning up at day care with women twenty years her junior, even the oldest of them did not appeal to her as a possible friend. Getting mistaken for the grandmother was going to be a regular thing. And hurt more each time it happened. Debbie asked herself why age was so important? Why couldn't she ignore it like some hippy friends of hers did? He was near sixty and she was in her fifties now and their latest had just started school. But that was them and besides, they had each other. They might be old but they were an old couple. Not an old single parent.

Debbie started the car and drove off. She drove down the road only because that was the direction in which the car was pointing, no other reason than that. Her mind processed the data needed to propel the vehicle whilst her soul wrestled with the dilemma she faced. Paul Gleeson was right. Look after yourself and give it some thought and the answer will make itself clear sooner or later. She only hoped it would be sooner than later. A cliché, but that was her life, more or less.

*****

"My husband still lives in my house. Out the back. He is so handy when it comes to looking after the kids if I have a date." Pete took in what the woman had just said but kept his own counsel. He couldn't imagine going home for a shag and meeting the ex the next morning at the breakfast table when he brought the kids in from crashing on his lounge floor.

"Some guys have a problem with it. But we don't". She went on. She? Glenda. "Sometimes we even have a great laugh over some of our respective dates. His or mine. I would say our relationship is so much better now we are divorced. We have had sex, I'll admit to that. Happened last New Years. Understandable I suppose, living so close, too much to drink, kids long asleep. Just forgot we were divorced, I guess."

Pete had had enough. "Look, it was nice meeting you. Thank you for the dance." No point beating around the bush. Get it over with. She looked like he had just grabbed her left tit, but he had truly had enough of her and her wonderful new relationship with the wanker she married in the first place. Amazing, some people.

Pete resumed his position near the bar, had to lean against the wall now as the place was a little more crowded and his table was taken. He looked back at Glenda just as another lothario sleazed into his still warm seat and leant nice and close to her. She was ok in the looks department. Body wasn't too bad and even the face not too wrinkled in this subdued lighting, given the fact she was three months older than Pete. He had some adjusting to do, that was for sure. Any young babe he looked at would look at him like some dirty old man, despite Hollywood's penchant for fifty plus male leads getting it off with twenty somethings. Dream on.

Pete was getting sick of this venue. It was a 'scene'. To Pete, it seemed everybody knew everybody else. As if they had worked through the regulars and waited vampire like for new blood. Men and women nodded at each other, even held animated conversations by the table load, all indicative they had been there, done that. Didn't work out so back to the Saturday night dance. Beats sitting at home, I suppose. But not by much. Not if what he had seen here tonight was anything to go by. Sure, some of the women seemed nice enough. Obviously first timers like him. The good ones came, saw and went. Any that came back a second time were slowly writing themselves off his maybe list. Too easy to end up like some of the regulars. Sad. Really sad, some of these people. And what else did they have in their lives? Lonely and alone, unable to form a relationship in the normal way, whatever that was. They resorted to the singles scene as a quick fix, only to find it sucked them in and kept them single and coming back for more. Why? It wasn't as if there were vast amounts of money being made here.

Pete finished off the last of his beer and placed the glass down in the center of a table nearby. One more look around and he was heading for the door. Twenty eight plus? Looked more like grab a granny night. He doubted a quarter of the people here were in their thirties, let alone late twenties. Ah well, it probably added a little spice to the anticipation felt by those who lacked the guts to risk pedophilia. What is it with this youth thing everybody had a hard on for? Personally Pete found young girls physically stimulating to look at but tiresome to talk to for anything more than a hello or goodbye.

Pete was more turned on by a well preserved mature woman in her thirties or even early forties. He felt sorry for those women who had come off second best to nature after birthing multiple children, or were too lazy to realise that more movement and less food might strip some of those wobbly layers off their butts and make them noticeable again. Of course it didn't change the beautiful inner person but Christ, be honest. If a guy had a choice between a woman in good physical shape and a slob, who would he pick? The same had to be said for guys, which made Pete want to run home and start working out again. He had to admit he had gotten a little lazy himself lately. And the lack of confidence that generated must have slowed him down tonight. Must have. Might as well stick around and get the supper he paid for, nothing worse than drinking on an empty stomach, even if you were watching how much you drank so you could still drive home. A taxi back to Whalan from here would cost a hundred bucks. He could get laid for that.

*****

Hamish and Clara sat looking somewhat dejected and forlorn. Their mother was lecturing them about the importance of telling the truth, not stealing and staying away from drugs. Given Clara was only just in school this last topic was a little above her but she gathered drugs were bad things and she vowed she would keep well away from them. Hamish knew drugs were run by guys with pony tails and dark skin and they used fast motor boats and planes and had guns. No way would he keep away from those guys if they ever set up shop in his school. He wouldn't take the drugs, no way. But he would like to run some, get a gun, maybe grow a ponytail. Yeah!

Nikki realised her lecture was losing some of its impact as Hamish started to give off that glazed far-away look he developed whenever he was off on another planet. Clara was obviously wrestling with some inner question of conscience. Ah well, leave it there for now. In fact, she had to think hard to recall the original infringement that had given rise to the lecture. Never mind, kept them on their toes to give them a little dressing down now and again. She dismissed them and watched as they bounced back into the here and now immediately. Amazing how that happens, she thought. Nikki turned as the kids ran out of the door leading to the verandah. At the door leading in from the hallway stood the man she had fallen totally in love with. Fast. Tim.

Wordlessly she crossed the carpeted space between them and draped her arms around his neck. Their lips met and began to live a life of their own. She felt her heat rising, burning like a flare and sending out those rescue me signals from her loins. He responded with the launch of his inflatable rescue boat. A rigid inflatable by the feel of it she thought. Reluctantly, knowing dinner would burn and children would starve she broke off the embrace.

"Hi" she said throatily.

"Hi yourself" was his reply.

"Can't wait."

"Me too."

They didn't have to explain to each other any further. They both meant the weekend. Not this one. The next one. The 'every second weekend' weekend that meant Hamish and Clara bonded with their biological father and his new, younger wife. And their two babies. Seemed everybody had a couple of kids somewhere. A kid or two from the first marriage, a kid or two from the second. Maybe first wife had one from before, maybe not. Second wife probably did. If anybody got to third wife then surely there were now at least, on average four kids, usually closer to eight in the immediate vicinity of any one breeding adult. That made for several brothers or sisters, numerous half and step brethren, handfuls of grand parents, aunts, uncles and volumes of cousins. For the modern nuclear family, mutating was the order of the day and Christmas must be an expensive nightmare of Biblical proportions.

Nikki was relieved Tim had no children from a previous marriage. No previous marriage, either. How novel. Tim found the step daddy thing immensely satisfying. An orphaned only child he had been brought up by a childless uncle and aunt. That was enough to raise some issues, but the uncles' personal attitude to every thing was irrationally aggressive and this had rubbed off on Tim. Not that he was all that aware that how he felt was not normal. How was he to know? Still, he enjoyed the attention the kids lavished on him. And the sex with Nikki was the best. Clara was only six, but she was already the dead spit of her beautiful mother. A few more years and she would be ripe for the plucking. Hamish was just about ready right now. Eight and big for his age, firm buttocks and thighs, smooth, hairless pubic area. Oh yeah. Soon, Hamish, my boy, soon. If it had been good enough for Uncle Steve with Tim then it was good enough for Tim with Hamish.

Tim gave Nikki one more, hungry kiss. The kind he would give to Hamish one night soon. And she wouldn't know a thing. And so what if she did? By then he would have her eating out of his hand. She needed him. He knew that. They both did.

*****

Terri finished what she was doing for John and walked straight into the bathroom without saying a word. John hated the way she did that. As if she was completing a chore she hated and couldn't wait to rinse away the displeasure. Pete had hated that habit of hers, too. But since she was the best at what she did he had learnt not to make any comment. John had also arrived at the same conclusion. Better to put up with it and focus on what went before.

John closed his ears to the bathroom sounds that confirmed her rejection of him in a manner words could never convey. It must be something personal he allowed, then promptly went back to other issues. The more he thought about it, the more it actually made sense. There was no way Debbie could bring the child up on her own. Not just from a financial point of view, but from the simple mechanics of rearing a child. They had done it with her two girls, John had been involved in that first hand and prided himself on his efforts at step-parenting. He was unaware the girls and Debbie used to laugh behind his back at his naïve attempts to be Mr Brady, without the three boys or Alice.

Terri came back in and cuddled up next to him as if she had never been away. She was truly unaware of how upsetting her habit was. Almost as if she had blanked out the walk to the bathroom, the spit and the rinse. Strange. Maybe she had witnessed something between her parents that affected her this way? John hadn't witnessed anything between his parents, at least not of that nature. He doubted they had done anything once he was on the scene and then he must have been either good luck or the one time in his life his father had ever drunk too much. Or his mother. They were both as puritanical as the other.

"Tomorrow you will speak to her, right?" Terri still refused to mention Debbie's name. Childish, but kinda cute at first.

"Yes, my sweet. I will be seeing her for lunch and I will make sure she realises how much better off the baby will be with us than with her. I know what to say." John comforted her.

Terri let herself drift off to sleep as she started to plan the colour of the nursery, the soft toys she would buy, the little baby clothes, everything nice and new. Not like when she was pregnant to Pete and his family kept giving her second hand stuff. Not clothes, but strollers, cribs, wash tables. Terri never seemed to recall how broke they had been then and that all the stuff was clean and in good repair. She just remembered the fact none of it was new. So what? Pete had argued. It worked the same as new stuff. Humph. Trust a man to not understand what it meant for a mother to have her own things for her first baby. Terri of course had never known the level of struggle Pete's parents had gone through when they were first married. She didn't realise that they were having a similar time and that every penny counted and the second hand things meant she had everything she would need and more. No, to Terri the only important thing was that these things, which were her right and she took them as such, were not brand spanking new. And that had hurt her. Not this time. This baby would have new things and John would be able to pay for them.

Terri fell asleep almost feeling the baby in her arms as she drifted away. Despite the part of her brain that was sharp as a razor and as cunning as a pack of foxes, Terri was still, deep in there somewhere, the loving natural mother Pete had fallen in love with so many years before. As she slept, almost as if her innocence returned by the very act of her alpha waves shutting down, she dreamt. Dreamt of babies, big houses, nurseries, shiny new prams and cots. And there, bouncing a beautiful baby on his knee was her husband. Pete. PETE. Terri woke with a start and realised she had only drifted off a few moments ago. She shook her head and tried to take up the dream where she left off. With all the goodies, but with someone else as her husband. Not necessarily John. Just not Pete. She couldn't handle Pete. Anyone but him. John would do, just not Pete. OK sub-conscious?

CHAPTER 13

Pete loosened his tie and undid the top button. Bugger it. He thought. Time to ditch the stupid thing. Ridiculous things, ties. Purely decoration. A throw back to the fops and cavaliers of the sixteenth century. Powdered wigs would be coming back any day now. The only practical use for ties, other than catching soup, was to wipe your sunglasses clean with. Pete took the offending article off and rolled it into a ball before finding a pocket to stuff it into.

He picked up his drink and wandered around the periphery of the dance, observing. He was not a part of this scene. He knew that. Never would be. It was so false, so contrived. As if being single once you had known the bounds of matrimonial paradise meant you were second rate, good only for this cobbled together attempt at changing your status. What about those guys who were the same age as him and had never married? Career women in the same boat? You didn't see them here. This place was so, so, so pedestrian.

No, those who had not been soiled by marriage kept themselves pure by mixing in similar untainted circles. The rest, well they hung out here. Tea and sympathy was what you'd get if this dance was held in the afternoon. Everyone hitting the scene for the first time still telling blow by blow accounts of the split, the property settlement hopes, the upcoming divorce. Those with all that under their belts would patrol the edges waiting the time to strike like a pack of sharks. Soon, the newbies would be absorbed into the group and they too would patrol the edges. They would recognise the signs of recent marital breakdown and smile inwardly now they were past all that.

Pete almost thought of them as vampires. Too scary to contemplate but once you have been bitten...... Once you, too, have the taste for blood….. Then it all seems so natural. Hell, he was letting this place get to him. Sure, it was a "scene". It certainly had a sub-culture that probably lived for each Saturday night, but what social grouping didn't? Fishing clubs were the same but without the disco lights. Lapidary clubs had their shakers and movers, the inner ring and the dabblers on the perimeter. Church groups had those who lived for the regular Sunday soiree and those who came when conscience and schedule allowed. This was no different. It was like a club or a congregation. In fact like any group of like-minded people clubbing together to promote their particular interest. In this case it was relationships.

But were they here to build new ones or lament the lost? Was it more important to be out and about, and to be seen to be out and about, then to actually change one's status from single to attached to married? What happened once a long term loner got lucky? That was obviously what those odd tables with obvious couples around them represented. Member made good. Back to flaunt it amongst the less fortunate. Look at me, I made it and so can you. It just takes persistence and three dozen chicken suppers.

Pete had had his chicken and two veggie supper. The guy in front of him was a vegetarian and Pete tried to get his quarter of chicken and give him his share of the veggies. The guy was all for it but not the tiny-minded cretin slapping out the vittles. Pete couldn't believe his attitude. Or his mentality. What did it matter to him if one guy got two helpings of chicken and another got two helpings of vegetables? Two dinners went out and two coupons were collected. The waiter was Asian, which explained his slavish adherence to his perception of right and wrong. No flexibility, Asians, Pete knew. From first hand experience he knew this. They had so much potential but would never really make it because they were too inflexible and couldn't compromise or think outside the circle. Ones and zeros just like computers. This is why they were so good at maths yet hadn't invented anything earth shattering in their entire history. Anything they did invent was never developed to its full potential unless some westerner had grabbed hold of it. Like fireworks. Took a European to turn a harmless crowd entertainment device like a firework into a refined lethal method of mass destruction.

Pete didn't think of himself as racist, he just called a spade a spade, as he saw it. He had travelled and seen a lot in his time and he understood the mentality of people like the waiter. He had seen the culture they had been born into and he understood their selfishness in looking after number one and damn anyone else. Those conditions did not breed an altruistic or philanthropic ethic. As things got better in Asia it would change. But for now it was all black or white unless you had the 'squeeze', the coffee money as some called bribes. Bribery was a way of life and not something to be ashamed of to many. Pete understood all this. But understanding didn't make accepting any easier. Especially since he was in his country, not theirs. He stepped down into the gutter to let locals past when he was in their country. Fair enough. But at home he expected a little more. Trouble was, he rarely got it as his countrymen were paranoid at being seen as racist. What is it about white people they feel they need to apologize for the colour of their skin all the time?

Pete pondered this and other dilemmas as he sipped his drink and wandered closer to the entrance. Or in his case, it was going to be the exit. He had had enough and he was ready to go home. Put his feet up, hit the stereo and relax. He didn't need this scene but it had been worth the fifteen bucks to get the education. It was at that point the doorman with English as his second language decided to take Pete to task for not wearing his tie.

"Excuse me, sir. You must keep your tie on whilst you are here" Very polite but the accent grated at Pete.

"Yes, well it's after nine o'clock and it was getting a bit tight." Pete fed him that line just to play the game a little.

"You must wear your tie the whole time or else you must leave, sir"

"Why? What's wrong with not wearing the tie? I meet the clubs dress regulations. Says nothing on the board about ties being compulsory." Pete threw that one in to confuse him a little more, make the guy think on his feet.

"You can go anywhere you like in the club but the auditorium is tie on for this event."

"What difference does it make if I have a tie on or don't have a tie on?"

"That is the rule, sir." the little guy was getting hot under the collar. Pete knew he could screw this guy around for a lot longer but he was bored with it. He could either make a big fuss and get thrown out, or simply leave. He gave the guy a hard stare that had the man take an involuntary step back. Without another word, Pete turned on his heel and walked straight out the door. His abrupt departure was an emotional letdown for the doorman, who had been pumping himself up for an altercation. He would be jumpy and spoiling for a fight to release the pent up emotion for the rest of the night. Pete knew this because he had been in the doorman's shoes. He had never enforced anything as blatantly archaic as a tie law. Wouldn't have even if he had been required to. It was something that begged for friction from the punters and he had enough to worry about without causing agro enforcing rules that had no basis in fact. How people dressed was no guarantee to how they would behave. He had seen the flashest dressed business wankers cause the most grief. Ah well, it was time to go anyway.

Pete went downstairs into the bar and picked out a poker machine. Not even able to be called one armed bandits anymore, the money went in in note form so there was no feeding of coins and no pulling of the handle. Simply press the button and let the computer do the rest. Quicker way of blowing your dough, if the truth be told. And Pete knew the management could adjust the payout probability of the machine. With these computerised ones they could probably do it remotely from a control room somewhere. Bastards. Then again, after the foreign waiter, short-arsed wog doorman and his stupid tie ethos and now loosing money at a rapid pace, Pete was not in the most benevolent of moods towards anyone. And definitely not at his most attractive for securing the attentions of the female of the species. Which is why, ten minutes later, he found himself leaving the club and heading for, well, not home. No. Pete was going to get laid. Even if he had to pay for it. Directly, that is.

*****

"You'll what?" Debbie was speechless. Dumbstruck. She ran the tape in her head one more time to replay what John had just told her. She still didn't believe what she had heard so she repeated her exclamation. "You will do what?""

"I will take the baby and bring him, or her, up and you can have reasonable access. Look Debbie," he placed a hand on each shoulder. "It's for the best. We both know that. You can't bring up a baby on your own. Christ, you are a grandmother. A baby will, well..." he left the rest unsaid but he knew he was scoring points with Debbie. She hadn't said anything about Terri yet. But she would. It was coming. He could feel it in his water.

"And Floppsy Moppsy? What'll she be doing with our baby?" Debbie showed her age and generation, as well as her New Jersey roots when she used such terms to refer to Terri. But how else could she mention her without saying 'that whore of a slut you're screwing John'?

"Terri will bring the baby up as if she was her own. I know she would make a great mother. Besides, you would have reasonable access and input on the child's welfare."

"What do you consider reasonable, John? Every birthday and one school holiday in every two?" Debbie was angry. Angry that Terri would play mommy to her child, with her husband. After she had gone through the pain of pregnancy that slut would get the easy bit. The admiring glances, the comments on how did she regain her figure so soon. Debbie was ready to vomit she was so strung out. But she was also old enough to know this might be her only option. At least the baby would have a chance. Two parents were better than one. She knew John was right: she could not handle bringing up the baby alone. But Christ it made her so damn angry. It was not fair. Dammit. Not fair.

"Look, " John started to skate around the access question. Terri had been adamant. 'Tell her anything but she has nothing to do with the baby once she spits it out. Nothing.' Terri had said. She meant it, too. John knew that. Christ, he was caught between the two of them. "Debbie, rest assured you will not want for anything. I will make sure you have the easiest pregnancy I can arrange" He actually believed he would have any influence on her pregnancy. Debbie almost laughed in his face. She knew what he meant. If he could throw money at the problem then it wasn't a problem anymore so there.

"What access, John?" Debbie knew he was negotiating around the issue. He had boasted to her often enough how he did that in deals for the company. This was just another deal to him. She wasn't going to let him negotiate his way around her. She wanted everything in writing, signed by him in front of her lawyer.

"Look" he said again, "The details can be worked out. I'll get Jerry onto it along with the property settlement. I have instructed him to let you keep Queensland." Not the whole state, of course. Just the house worth three quarters of a million and rising. Calculated loss. Give up the biggie and hold on to all the little things that ended up worth more. That was Jerry's strategy and Jerry was the best lawyer in town. This way he kept Terri appeased, got the kid for her and held onto the Sydney house, the car, the stocks and a few other things. Debbie got the Queensland house and all its furniture, plus a lot of the Sydney stuff. Who cares? Terri wanted to buy all new stuff anyway. And the real estate market was heading up. Now was the time to invest. Shit, they were throwing money at him all the time. Everyone from American Express to his broker had money begging to be borrowed. Interest rates? So damn low you could jump over them with no legs, his broker had said. Whatever that meant. No, he wasn't losing here. Far from it.

Debbie turned and looked John in the eye. "Queensland? You'll give me Queensland? You swore you would never give me Queensland." Debbie was suspicious but still, greed could override all the other emotions.

"I know. It breaks my heart but I have to be fair. I know that Debs." He sounded like a little lost schoolboy. If that didn't work every time on Debbie then she would have instantly seen the red flag waving in the air. But, she was a sucker for that little lost schoolboy. Always had been. She started to relax. Listen to what he said. It made sense. She came off ok.

Yeah, why couldn't they be adult about this whole thing. He still cared for her. It had just happened. Yes, ok. The baby would be better off with him. She'd have reasonable access. John weaved his magic spell over her as he had in the past. She sat back, listening to him crooning all the things she desperately wanted to hear, deep down. He knew what he was doing. She knew what he was doing. Despite all the hurt and pain, even the toughest of us sometimes just wants to lie back and let ourselves be led, be taken care of. It's why we believe things then that seem so reasonable, so right. Only when examined in the cold light of day, with twenty twenty hindsight do we see the fatal flaws. And by then, as Debbie would find out soon enough, it was too late.

*****

Tim finished masturbating and cleaned himself off. He unlocked the bathroom and walked out, hearing his "family" downstairs. Hamish was playing on his Nintendo, Clara was teasing the dog and Nikki was cooking. Tim had been fantasizing about what it would be like to take Hamish. Just like his Uncle Steve had taken him. He had hated it at first, cried a lot. The pain. But then, afterwards he realised it was their little secret. It was something only he and Uncle Steven shared. Then the pain wasn't so bad. Then he started to look forward to the visits. The soft foot steps in the hall. The pause at the door, the listening for his breathing. The slow turning of the doorknob and the cautious pushing open of the door. Tim would hold his breath in anticipation, already erect and aroused.

He paused at the top of the stairs and enjoyed the rest of the recollection but stopped short of going as far as when his voice started to break. It had stopped then. Uncle Steve didn't come any more. Tim had been devastated, as if he was ugly now he was becoming a man. Later he understood. Now he agreed. But at the time he had been so angry he had told his Aunt Mary. She had slapped his face and told him not to be such a disgusting little boy. Uncle Steve had come to him that night. Hadn't he. If only to say goodbye for ever. Tim understood. And then Aunt Mary had gone away. Just like that. No note. Nobody said anything about it. Nothing. It just wasn't talked about. Simple as that.

*****

Nikki looked up from her cooking and saw her man at the top of the stairs, deep in thought if the look on his face was anything to go by. He saw her watching him and smiled at her. She smiled back. She felt safe, comfortable. At home. It was good to have a man around the house again. She had missed that. So had the children. Especially Hamish. Boys needed a role model, someone to look up to.

Tim saw Nikki watching him and he smiled. Soon, sweet Nikki. Soon I'll let Hamish enjoy what I had with my uncle. Something special, just between us. Boys need that. A kind of, well, role model he guessed. Tim had heard the expression and thought he knew what it meant. It was just the context he had trouble with.

CHAPTER 14

Alena knew she had an hour, hour and a half tops if she was lucky. No time to waste because he would be back any moment now. And if he caught her… Well, he just better not catch her. Simple as that. No second chances. If this didn't work he would beat her so bad it would be months before she could even think of escaping again. And he wouldn't give her another chance like this. She raced around grabbing clothes and toys and stuffing them into bags and knowing she had too much and couldn't carry it all by herself. Not all this stuff and two little kids, a stroller and god knows what else.

Alena wasn't the brightest of girls, but she wasn't stupid, either. Possessed with a common sense motherhood was hardly responsible for she trimmed down the load to the very barest of essentials. The other, more important items she threw into a couple of large carrier bags for Wendy to pick up and keep for her. Wendy knew she was running today. She had offered to take Alena and the kids to the station but Alena had knocked back her offer. If he knew she was involved with her escape, he would…..Shit!. He might kill her! He'd already tried to kill Alena. That had been the last straw. That had done it. Holding the pillow over her head whilst he screwed her when he was drunk and she didn't want sex was one thing. She could live with that. But the knife had left a scar. A thin red line, sure, but still he had marked her. Next time? Well next time he might press harder on the blade and cut her throat.

Alena tried to busy herself with packing to rid her head of the memory of how that knife had felt, pressed against her throat while Jacky and Kayleen had looked on. Too young to know anything other than mummy was crying. He had laughed at that. Did his thing, zipped up and walked into the lounge to fall asleep in front of the TV. She had picked up the knife and felt like cutting his dick off but she knew she couldn't do it. Not in cold blood. And he hadn't always been like this. Not at first. At first he had been so nice. Jacky had just been born and she was fifteen and all alone and needed somewhere to live.

He had been like the father she had never really known. Thirty three. Single with an ex missus and a kid somewhere. Alena had felt like a proper missus when he took her to the club for tea. She had been his woman and proud of it. But that had worn pretty thin when he started the hitting. Little slaps at first. Then full on punches. She had deserved some of them, she knew that. She had nagged and nagged, the baby needed this or that and sure it wasn't his baby but she didn't know what else to do. So he had smacked her, wasn't enough to make her want to end up on the street again. Alone.

Then when she was pregnant with his kid she thought he would be happy. Change even. Change? Fat chance! He had been down the pub with his Dad when the baby was born. She had had her second caesarian and all alone again. Just like the first time. Only now she was seventeen and no longer a ward of the state. Now she had to fend for herself. Remembering her status made her look longingly at her TV, video, washing machine. All appliances the social woman had gone shopping with her for when she left the state school and moved out.

Then she had fallen pregnant with Jacky and the father had done a runner as soon as she told him. Not quite straight away. First he had told her to get an abortion. Even offered to help pay for it. His idea of being a responsible adult, she supposed. Not bad given he was the same age she was. But abortion was out for Alena, wasn't it? Hadn't she just spent seven years in the Catholic school system as a ward of the state because her Dad and step mother couldn't handle her? Hadn't her real mum been a catholic? No, actually she hadn't been. It was her step mother who was the catholic.

Still, seven years of indoctrination and a teenage mother to be meant she wasn't thinking all that straight. And Jacky was such a nice boy. And now she had Kayleen she was making twice what he got on the dole. He would feel the pinch when he wanted drinking money on an off pay week now she was going. He couldn't claim any of her pension, could he? No, surely not. No, Wendy had told her the money was hers for the kids and she shouldn't let him blow it on booze. Wendy didn't know him, obviously. OR his right hook.

Alena's sense of humour was quite developed given the patchy nature of her formal schooling. In fact, there were a number of qualities held by Alena that made her stand out in a crowd. Her firm young body, hardly touched by two recent births was one feature that stood out. The way she had sprung back into shape after the last one was proof, if any was needed, of nature's intention in making children sexually capable long before they were mentally able to handle parenting. Of course, when Mother Nature put her idea of a human race together, she was under the impression the tribe would help in the rearing of the young. As the tribe made way for the nuclear family things weren't too bad. But once modern reality sunk in and single parenting by teenage girls became the rule rather than the exception in some societies, day to day living didn't have time for nature to play catch up and give the girl a fighting chance. Consequently, the term "ill-equipped" made new sense.

Alena was a child herself. A child who had been denied a proper childhood by a mother who had died too young, and a father who had found it all too hard and given in to the selfish jealousy of a new wife bent on giving it all to her own flesh and blood. Instead of time to adjust to being without a mother, Alena had been subjected to the hatred of a woman who had virtually never grown up herself, her own children birthed during breaks from her career as a school teacher. School Teacher? The perennial child. Spends twelve years at school, leaves and goes to school for three or four years to learn to be a teacher, then promptly goes to school for the next thirty or forty years and never learns what life is like in the real world. Teachers live in a world where they are the center of attention. They stand out the front of the class, they are listened too, referred to. They mould young minds and are used to being obeyed, even if it is by people younger and less mature than themselves. And they think this is the real world. So it was no wonder Alena turned out as she did, a mass of neuroses trying to escape from a man too old for her own good and too thick for his.

*****

"Put an ad in the local paper. That's what I do." Chris said between sips of his beer.

"Ad? What kind of ad?" Pete asked, sipping his own beer as punctuation.

"Mate, it works like a charm. I put an ad in the paper for a flat mate and then I interview the respondents. If I haven't got her in the cot within thirty minutes of her coming over for the interview, no way she gets the room." Chris emphasized how easy it was with a final swig, then reached for another coldie as he tossed the empty bottle to one side.

The two men were sitting around the garden table in Pete's backyard, the remains of a BBQ lunch lying about in mute testament to the truth that men can cook and do make the best chefs. Not too big in the salad department but KFC handled the extras. The main course, charred cow flesh, was cooked to perfection by Pete and eaten with gusto by both of them.

"So what do I say? 'Woman wanted for casual sex on live in basis?' That probably wouldn't even get printed."

"Don't be a drongo! Keep it simple but obvious. Target your market mate." Chris replied.

"OK, how about this?" Pete read off his suggested ad copy and Chris beamed.

"Perfect mate. Absolutely perfect. If that doesn't get you laid, nothing will. Come on, let's phone it in, no point wasting time." Chris led the way inside to Pete's office and the phone, carrying the week old copy of the same local newspaper they would run the ad in.

*****

"Debbie, are you sure? Are you one hundred percent certain this is what you want to do?" Jerry the family lawyer asked her for what had to be the fifth time.

"Yes. Yes. Yes already! Jerry, look at me. I'm too old to be a single mom. I'm nearly as old as you are. John has run off with some Floppsy Moppsy whore and I am in the club. Alone. What do you expect me to do? I have two kids already. I can't face bringing this one up alone, not knowing John is off with his whore. No way, Jerry. Come on. Do your job. Draw up the agreement." Debbie finished saying what she had to say and turned away to look out the office window of her long time family attorney. Jerry shook his head but knew she was right. He didn't like it but that wasn't his decision to make, or his place to say so.

"OK. I'll do as you ask. I will make sure you get visitation…." Debbie cut him off mid sentence.

"No. No Jerry. Don't. No visitation, I couldn't stand it. I'm leaving as soon as the baby is born and handed over. Back to the States. I've had enough. I need a complete break, a total change of scenery. I thought about it and I think, no I know it's the right thing to do. For the best." She seemed to grow another inch as she said that. Jerry could see she had not only made up her mind, she was feeling good about doing it too. She was taking control again. Taking back her life, her choices, making some hard decisions and living with them.

"Good for you Debs. I'll give you a call when the paperwork's ready to sign. It makes no difference to the courts but do you want to sign with John, or separately,?"

"Separately Jerry. I have seen the last I want to see of John Taylor. When he left the other night I realised he was right about the baby but I realised one other thing too. He had made his new bed and he was lying in it, I had better make mine or I'll never get a good night's sleep ever again, you know what I mean, Jerry?"

Jerry knew exactly what she meant. He had made that choice himself fifteen years ago when his first wife left him. And again three years ago when he left his second wife. How long before he made that choice again, he didn't know. What he did know was it got easier every time. If he married a fourth time he would probably qualify as either a serial monogamist or a wedding cake addict.

Debbie smiled at the man she had known for two decades and looked out his office window at the harbour. It was for the best. Best for her. Best for the baby. Best for John. Too damn bad it was probably best for the floozy, too.

*****

"It's yours." John said over the phone.

Terry said nothing. Too stunned. What did he mean? Surely not? Not this easy? Not the baby?

"Honey did you hear what I said?" John's voice had the imperious tone of authority it took on whenever he rang from his office, high in the corporate tower overlooking the harbour. Not like how he could whine like a little boy when he was in their bed. At work he was the man, The Man! The number three in a global group that counted its monthly income in tens of millions and soon would up that to billions.

"That is super!" Terry quickly composed herself and her thoughts. John's office tone had that effect on her. She liked it. Made him the man she wanted him to be. She wasn't a fan of his little lost puppy side. No attraction there for her whatsoever. Man. Manly. Power. In charge. That got her juices flowing. "When John? When will we have our baby?"

"Another four months, maybe less if it is premature but let's hope it goes full term for the baby's sake. " John was already wanting to wind this call up. He had work to do. "Terry, I'll see you tonight. Meet me at Mario's' at seven, we'll celebrate, ok?"

"OK. I'll wear the new dress, the white one. And the pearls. I love you." Actually she meant she loved the dress and the pearls.

"Bye. Love you too." The last three words were said sotto voce as the 3 o'clock appointment had just been ushered in by his secretary. John hung up the phone and wiped any domestic thoughts from his mind as he wound up to speed for the Beverley Hills project. The L.A. broker was being introduced to him, assuring him he had enjoyed the flight and so on, small talk fading away, getting down to business. Baby, Debbie, even Terry, all forgotten.

*****

Hamish sobbed. He was scared. So scared. Too scared to say anything or do anything. He liked Tim. But not like this. This was not right. He cried. Tears streamed down his cheeks as Tim's hand fondled his genitals. He was aroused, he couldn't help it and in his innocence he felt guilt and shame and didn't have the capacity to know he was not to blame.

Tim sobbed. He was scared. Very scared. Nikki might walk in on him at any moment. He had left her sleeping soundly but she might wake up. What if Hamish cried out? He had told him it was their special secret. That if he told his mum he would be punished. Of course he wanted it, couldn't he see he was aroused? Didn't that prove he was a bad boy? Don't bad boys get punished? Not if they keep their secrets. Tim will protect him. Keep him safe from harm and punishment. Just say nothing and all will be well. Tears of ecstasy seeped down Tim's cheeks. He was aroused, so aroused. So hot. So hard. But not tonight. Not this time. Just get him ready. Get him primed and ready. Get him guilt ridden and trapped. No more. Not just yet.

Tim shuddered as the orgasm erupted in his loins, just from touching Hamish! Just touching alone and he had made it. He was that ready for the boy. Hamish followed a few seconds later. He couldn't help it. He just couldn't. It was wrong. It was his fault. He actually liked how good it felt now it was done. He prayed Tim would keep his word and not tell his mother. He prayed.

Tim stroked his forehead and bid him to sleep with a finger to his lips. He prayed he would say nothing. He wasn't yet fully in control of Nikki but he couldn't wait any longer. The lust was too strong, he knew he had to make a move. It worked, though. It worked. He got off, Hamish got off. He knew he would say nothing. But just in case, he would pray he would say nothing too. Might as well get all the help he could.

*****

"Male, Female, Single Mum with 1 or 2 kids OK to share house, own room, $100 a week, call…" Alena was already dialing even before she started to read out the number in the ad. Sounded perfect. So many share accommodation places had hung up as soon as she said she had two little kids.

The phone started to ring at the other end and she twisted the curly phone cord absent mindedly as she waited for the advertiser to pick up. She felt a sudden desperation as she wondered if the room was already taken. The newspaper came out that morning but she had rung before on the day of publication to find whatever it was being advertised had already been sold. Not sure how that worked but she prayed it wouldn't happen with the room.

"Hello?" A strong male voice answered the phone before she realised the ringing had even stopped.

"Hello, I'm calling about the share accommodation, single mum with kids ok? Is the room still available? I'm finding it really hard to find somewhere to live because I have two small kids, one is two and the other one is six months, well he'll be two next month just before my birthday." Alena couldn't stop herself gushing, she really wanted the room that much.

"Wait a moment. Look, the room is still here, you are the first to call but we need to meet and see if you like the place and if we can get along and so on first, ok?" She liked the sound of his voice. Strong, manly. In charge.

"Sure, OK, when can I come around? My Dad finishes work at six, he's a courier, he said he can bring me around to look at the place, will you promise not to let it go to anyone else before I get a look please?"

The voice on the other end gave a chuckle that told her she wouldn't have to worry. "Yeah, come around at six, I won't make a decision until we meet even if Bo Derek comes first."

"Bo who? Never mind. I will be there, I promise. Thanks, bye." She hung up and shrieked with joy. Then she shrieked with anguish as she realised she didn't have the address. She hit redial and held her breath as the phone automatically redialed the last number rung and then she heard a ring at the other end before the phone was picked up. Before she could say anything she heard that strong voice reading out the address. He said it twice and she took it down. She hung up still hearing that cute chuckle in the earpiece.

Alena couldn't wait for six o'clock but she had no other way to get there by herself. The place was several suburbs away and she had to look after her kids until her step mother came home from work or her dad got there. She started to pack a few loose things in her battered bags, no point leaving it to the last minute and she just had to get this place. She would do anything to get the place, anything. She had spent two weeks now, hiding at her dad's house and cramped into a room with her two kids and her youngest half sister. She needed her own place. She had to have her own place by next month. She was going to be eighteen then. Grown up. An adult. No way she wanted to be living with dad and the step-mum then. No way. Bo who?

CHAPTER 15

"Mrs Taylor. Mrs Taylor, wake up. The doctor is here to talk to you. About your baby. Wake up Mrs Taylor."

Debbie could hear the nurse's voice, feel her light but insistent touch on her shoulder but really she didn't feel like responding. She hurt. The anesthetic had worn off, if they actually gave her any. Her stomach felt as if they had cut her open, ripped out her baby and then sewn her back up again. Which is exactly what had happened.

"Mrs Taylor, Debbie, wake up." It was a man's voice. The doctor. Debbie gave up trying to ignore the voices and the pain and opened her eyes. The doctor stood beside her bed, the nurse stood a little behind him, looking worried. Yes, it was a worried look on her face. More obvious than a mere look of concern. This was a worried look. What could be wrong now, she wondered?

"Debbie, the baby is alive and kicking and in the incubator and we will let you see him soon. I'm sorry but it is as bad as we feared, just as we discussed before you went into labour." The doctor paused for effect and to give the news time to seep in past the last dregs of whatever it was the anesthetist had given her when he operated.

"What do you mean, how bad?" Debbie asked, giving the doctor his cue to proceed. She was awake now and able to take in what he had to tell her. No point waiting any longer, might as well tell her and get it over with so she can move on.

"Your baby has cerebral palsy. We can't tell to what degree at this stage but I can tell you it will be a very advanced stage and he will need personal care for the rest of his life. I'm talking everything from feeding him to cleaning to toilet visits, everything. I know you didn't want to discuss the details when we first knew something was wrong during your pre-natal checkups but you have to face this at some stage and really, now is as good a time as any." The doctor had known for some time the extent of the baby's disabilities but his patient had simply refused to concern herself, didn't seem to care. Not one iota. It was strange. No, it was bizarre.

"That's ok doc, my husband and his floozy will be adopting the baby within 24 hours. Its their problem." With that, Debbie rolled away towards the window and closed her eyes. She started to cry, couldn't help it. Part of her wanted her baby, part of her was relieved it was all over and part of her wanted to die.

Bringing up a severely handicapped baby would be a struggle at the best of times, even if she were twenty years younger and had the support of her husband. But to even think of attempting it at her age and on her own was ridiculous. In a way she was somehow glad the baby would be handed over to John and his whore. He was their problem now. They wanted her child and they could have him.

Jerry had written an iron clad contract that there was no way they could wriggle out from. John was contractually, legally bound to provide that baby with the very best his mega salary could offer until the child turned 23, if he wanted to go to college. He could not refuse to accept the child regardless of condition, his only escape clause had been if the baby had been stillborn. That hadn't happened. The baby had been premature but still it was born alive. Alive yet facing a life of arguable quality.

Cerebral palsy, perhaps one of life's cruelest afflictions. Inside the child knows what's going on and lives like anyone else. But outside. Outside they hunch and dribble and moan and groan and have difficulty telling people they aren't stupid. They aren't dumb. They have a communication and coordination problem.

Well, John and his whore now face the rest of their lives looking after a child that can't walk, can't talk and can't do anything for itself. Debbie had known for months now, but she kept it to herself. Why spoil the surprise? Surprise bitch! You wanted my baby well you got him. A son and heir for John. Be proud.

The doctor looked at his patients' curved back and then turned to the nurse, giving her some instructions for sedation and pain killers. He didn't understand his patient's reaction but then at her age, who knows? He did know there was more to the story than he was aware of. Too bad, he was too busy to waste any more mind space on this drama. He had a ward full of women and their babies who fitted into the accepted mould of new mum and child and he was only half way through his rounds. If he wanted to finish up and make it to the staff canteen before the food went cold again he'd better pull his finger out.

*****

125

Alena pushed back against his thrusts, she moaned and made little mewling noises like she had seen the porn stars do on those videos she had watched with her last lover. Pete was different. He didn't watch porn videos. He lived them. Whenever they did it they did it like some movie. Against the door frame, over the bathroom sink, halfway across the bedroom doorway on the floor as if their lust couldn't wait to make it to the double bed.

She fought against the ties he had used to strap her to the bed posts. It was a metal four poster but the mozzie net was gone. Got too dusty and Pete couldn't be bothered cleaning it so he threw it away. It had too many holes in it from where the cats had scrambled over it anyway, When there had been cats in the house. She'd taken the cats. Left him the dogs. Now he had Alena.

Their sex was wild, lusty and debauched. Anything goes, anything went. Alena was game for anything, it was just about all new for her. She took it every way he offered it and he offered it to her every way there was.

"Pete!" his mate Chris had said one day shortly after she moved in. "No way will this last. She's seventeen for shits' sake!" Chris was probably more jealous than worried.

"Chris!" Pete replied. "It's not supposed to last! This is my therapy. I need this. I know it won't last but while it does I'm going to enjoy it. She's legal."

Legal then and more so now. She was eighteen. Old enough to vote. Old enough to drink, legally anyway. Old enough for Pete to enjoy, knowing each time might be his last chance to get his load off with a pretty young thing half his age and twice as horny.

Alena loved Pete. She loved any man who gave her the attention her father never had. She loved Pete because he was older, just like the last guy and no doubt the next. It was her thing. Besides, older guys lasted longer, knew more and cared for her, not like the young blokes she had done it with. Wham bang forget even thank you mam they were already gone.

She screamed as she came but she didn't care. Her kids were gone. Adopted out. Or soon would be. She had spent the last four months going through the psyche tests and having the social worker convince herself it was for the best. Pete had kept right out of it, her call. He had told her it had nothing to do with him and whether she kept the kids or not made no difference, one day probably soon they would split and she would find someone else.

Pete had spoken to the social worker and the psychologist lady about the adoption of Alena's two kids. He wanted them to make triply sure she wasn't doing it out of some misguided idea she had to to keep hold of Pete. He had seen both women react to the admission they were slamming each other. He knew they were disgusted, or disappointed. One or the other. Maybe both. Screw them.

Pete didn't care what they thought of him so long as they did their court appointed duty and made sure he wasn't the reason she was adopting out her kids. They were nice kids, aren't they all at that age? He hadn't gotten too close to them on purpose. Only make things harder for everyone.

He had taken Alena to the psyche appointments, and the social worker and even when the kids were handed over to an interim foster carer. Nice lady. When Alena went to meet the prospective adoptive parents he made sure he was unavailable. Not his business. Didn't want to know.

Alena didn't adopt her kids because of Pete. She had thought about it when the first one came along. She was young and naïve but not stupid. She knew the enormity of her decision. She did it to give her kids the best chance in life she could. What could she offer them? Family life? Two different fathers, one young and dumb and nowhere to be found and the other older and dumber and violent with it?

Even if she met and married a man as good as Pete and she knew he wasn't going to be with her for the long haul, then what? The kids would still have some contact with their fathers, somehow. No, far better they go to a childless couple who are screaming out to be parents and then the biological father hasn't a hope. Better for the kids. Better for her. New life. At eighteen, just when life should be starting. New life. An entire life over with. New life. New man. Pete will go one day she knew, but until then, might as well enjoy him.

*****

Nikki pushed back against his thrusts, she moaned and made little mewling noises like she had seen the porn stars do on those videos she had watched with her last lover. Tim was different. He didn't watch porn videos. He lived them. Whenever they did it they did it like some movie. Against the door frame, over the bathroom sink, halfway across the bedroom doorway on the floor as if their lust couldn't wait to make it to the double bed.

She fought against the ties he had used to strap her to the bed posts. They were only short and he had tied the knots so tightly they were starting to hurt. His thrusts were getting harder and more forceful. He grabbed her hair and pulled her head back. Hard. He rammed himself against her so hard her head hit the wall. Hard. It hurt but she felt her orgasm taking over like an aphrodisiac anesthetic.

Even as the waves of pleasure washed away he kept hammering her as if he couldn't reach the place she had just left. Hard. Harder. Hammer. Again. It was starting to hurt. Really hurt. Pain. She cried. She cried out. She told him it hurt. He wouldn't stop. Harder. Harder. He hammered home until her head was banging against the wall in a rhythmic tattoo. She screamed and he tensed. Stopped. Relaxed. Collapsed. Over.

Nikki lay still, glad the pain was going away. Tim lay still, then slowly she felt him move. Soft, rhythmic sobbing. He was crying. She tried to roll over to comfort him but her bonds kept her face down with the three pillows under her tummy still pushing her butt in the air. The pillows slewed sideways from under her as she half turned and asked him what was wrong, was he alright, what was the matter all in one breath and half a sentence.

Tim looked at her, his face in line with hers as he lay to one side, half on and half off of her. He snarled, slapped her hard then got up and left the room. Nikki was stunned. Totally taken aback. What the hell?

*****

Terri pushed back against his thrusts, she moaned and made little mewling noises like she had seen the porn stars do on those videos she had watched with her last lover. John was different. He didn't watch porn videos. He had seen maybe one in his entire life time. Terri had seen more. Lots more. She had starred in one. Well, a home porno movie anyway. One of her first boyfriends. A life time ago. Before John. Before Pete. Before just about everybody.

He fought against the ties she had used to strap him to the bed posts. Seemed like the only way to get him to fuck her lately was to ambush him and tie him to the bed. She was horny. Turned on. So what if she was having her periods. Made it better for her. Hot. Hotter. She needed it now. So what was blood? Just another bodily fluid like spit or cum. She was safe. No AIDS. Slap on the K-Y and go for it. Damn she needed it.

Tomorrow. Big day. Pick up the baby. John had told her the baby was born that afternoon, or just before lunch, better get it right. Need those details for the horoscope. Terri was getting into horoscopes. Not much else to do. No job, stuck at home all day most days of the week waiting for the big executive to remember he had a wife waiting for him. They didn't eat out as often as they used to. He was always working late but at least she knew he really was working late and not just lying to her like he lied to the old cow.

Tomorrow. She would have her baby. That would keep her busy. Still hadn't found the right Nanny even though she must have interviewed the entire stock of Nannies on the Australian sub-continent. Maybe she should get an English Nanny. Advertise in The Times. Something to brag about to the other wives.

Tomorrow. Can't wait. Go to the hospital, meet the lawyer and the official from the adoption authority or whoever Jerry said she was and sign the release, then take her baby home. Maybe stop off for a coffee on the way. Show her friends. They were dying to see the baby. Absolutely agog with anticipation. Couldn't wait. Tomorrow.

*****

Hamish pushed back against his thrusts, he moaned and made little mewling noises that came from the depths of his tortured prepubescent soul. Tim pushed harder and harder, his grip on the boy's hair pulling his head back, compressing his spine and making his mouth gape.

He was bleeding, hurt, wounded, torn body, torn pride. Nothing left. No dignity. He cried. He screamed. He heard his mother in her room scream in reply. Heard her shriek of terror that rang through to the core of his being, that primal umbilical cord of the mind still unbroken and never to part until and perhaps even beyond the death of one or both of them.

Tim exploded, far easier and sooner than he had or ever would with Nikki. Hamish was real. Hamish was the truth. Hamish was pure and everything that made life worth living. Everything else was preparation or obstruction or mere distraction. But not Hamish. Hamish was what his life was all about. His purpose. He loved Hamish. Loved him. Truly. No woman could love him so purely. So rightly. As God intended them to love. Man and Boy.

Hamish felt pain. Shame. Humiliation. Agony. The physical and the emotional and the spiritual wounds ran together in the blood that flowed down the back of his thighs and collected in pools behind his knees then eased over the side of his legs to the once pure white sheets on which he lay. Even the withdrawal was painful. Abrupt. Unexpected. Welcomed yet hurting.

Tim rolled off of Hamish and lay on his back, staring at the bedroom ceiling. Naked, bloodied, semen stained. Satiated. Happy. Ecstatic.

*****

Nikki was free. Her wrists bled but she was free from her bonds. She picked up the bed end, or what was left of it and hefted it in her hand. Not heavy enough. She knew instinctively she needed something with more weight. If she were to do what had to be done, she needed more weight. Or sharper. She saw her bedside table drawer was ajar. She knew the other bedside table had a scissor in the drawer. The same pair she had used last night to cut out the pages for her scrapbook. She rolled back across the bed as she heard a crude sound come from her son's bedroom.

She opened the drawer and her hand closed around the handle of the large scissors as she figured out what the sound was. Sobbing. The sobbing of a boy not yet old enough to grow hair under his armpits. Her son. Her son and her lover. Her ex-lover. The sodomiser of her son. And her. Only she had consented. Hamish hadn't.

Nikki stood up and clenched the scissors in her hand like she had seen in countless Hollywood horror movies. Only this wasn't a movie. It was real. Her life. Her son's life. In her home.

CHAPTER 16

"No Way! No Fucking, freaking way! No way are we taking that…that…that thing into our house!" Terri was really losing it John thought. In front of everybody here at the hospital. He could see the looks of disgust on their faces. Alright for them, they didn't have to take the baby home.

"John, I am not going to be a mother to a freak show. Look at that thing. Can't you and that old slag get anything right? Jesus!" Terri let it all out. She was so angry. She had looked forward to this moment all her life. Her own baby. A baby to love, to hold, to cuddle, to caress, to take care of. Not….not this….this thing…this freak show.

Terri turned away from the incubator. She had refused to hold the baby when the midwife offered him to her. She just couldn't bring herself to hold such a misshapen, twisted creature. She wanted to retch, to cleanse herself of the disgust she felt, so powerful she was getting reflux, her expensive lunch coming back to haunt her.

John turned away and looked at the back of his girlfriend, soon to be wife but not yet officially fiancé. He knew there was no way Terri would change her mind. He had seen it in her eyes. He had seen something else too at that moment. John wasn't stupid. Stupid didn't get you to the number three spot in a global organization like his. From nowhere, before you hit 35. Stupid he wasn't.

John didn't know what it was he had seen but he did know he didn't like it. It scared him. Maybe it was meant to. The female of the species is an underrated animal, he knew that. He also knew the protective instincts of a mother defending her young could be terrible to behold if on the receiving end. But Terri had no maternal bond to protect her from any feelings of revulsion. Actually, those feelings were there to protect the defenceless new born from being abandoned.

He didn't know what it was, deep in her soul and leaking out in venomous light rays from her eyes, but he knew it was evil. Pure and simple. He realized it right there and then. In the maternity ward of the hospital where his misshapen, cerebral palsy suffering son lay. She had evil in her. Despite the beauty, the love, the warmth and the wonderful, generous side to her he had enjoyed first hand for all of these months. Despite all that, she had evil in her.

He had known it all along, or pretty well all along. It excited him. Scared him but excited him. She had the mean streak he wanted but the best he could muster was garden variety nasty. He wasn't a real villain, even though he had foreclosed a few people's homes and businesses and although scared of their anger he enjoyed the power. But not real evil.

Terri had it. He knew, he just knew. She had that rod of steel in her backbone that could drive a man to do her bidding, even though he would know it was wrong. He wouldn't be able to help himself. Not unless he was very strong. Pete was strong enough. John wasn't. He knew that, just knew it somehow. Terri was evil, deep down and now she had let it out, just for a moment. He had seen it. Deep inside the real her. He never wanted to glimpse that inner part of her ever again. But he did, though, didn't he? He wanted to see it again. He wanted her to scare him. He liked it. Like when she tied him to the bed and teased him. Then fucked his brains out. And he was helpless to stop her, not that he wanted her to stop. Even when she started to hurt him. Even then.

Terri walked out of the ward, down the hall and pressed the button to summon the lift. She wanted a cigarette. She wanted to throw up. She wanted to murder that slag. She wanted her baby. Not that.......that thing. She would be a laughing stock. No, not even those who would pity her with their fawning attention would do it. She didn't need pity, she was too strong willed to need pity. She wanted their respect, their adoration, admiration. Fat chance she'd get it with that crippled piece of shit. Damn, where's the friggin' lift.

The bell bonged and the floor number lit up, the elevator door opened and she stepped in just as John caught up with her and entered the lift car at the same time. She looked at him and told him not to say a damn word without saying a word herself. He took the hint and obeyed her. Always did, the creep. Damn she felt nothing but disgust and contempt for him, the baby, the world. Shit!

*****

"You made me give up my kids." Alena spat the accusation at Pete. She spat some spittle at him along with the cruel and totally incorrect allegation. She knew Pete had nothing to do with her decision to have her two kids adopted out. But acknowledging that required some part of her brain being used for rational thought and right now she needed it all for emotion.

Pete wasn't going to argue with her, pointless at this stage of her rage. She was all venom and spite and they both knew she was angry at herself but she just couldn't accept that. She needed someone to blame and Pete was the one. The closest in more than just geographical terms. They say you always hurt the ones you love the most and she did love Pete. As much as she had ever been able to love anyone in her eighteen years of life.

"If it wasn't for you I would still have my kids." Alena tried again to rekindle the dying embers of her anger. Pete just walked into the living room and switched the TV on, then sat down on the couch. Alena followed him, still spoiling for a fight but running out of things to say.

"Come here. Sit down and talk to me, Alena." Pete held out a olive branch that Alena let hover in mid air between them for just long enough to show she was still angry and yet not so long he'd change his mind.

She sat on the couch and curled into a ball of sobs, cuddled up to Pete and let him swallow her up into his protective arms. It was over between them. She knew that. That was what had set her off this time. She knew it had to have been coming ever since their first night together. Always happened. Her fault. Just like why her Mum died in the car accident, her Dad married that shrew of a step mother of hers and her life now was screwed. All her fault. Her kids gone, her fault. Everything was her fault.

"Hey, cheer up. You know you gave your kids up because it was the best thing for them. You know that because the social worker made very sure you knew that was the reason. You know you had discussed it with your social worker in Grafton before you even came down to Sydney. So let it go, it's done. Over. Move on Alena."

Pete's advice made sense, or at least it would later when she calmed down a little more. At least he wasn't kicking her out, just telling her the sex was over. The boyfriend/girlfriend thing. Finished. Fine, she'd find someone else to screw. Just so long as he was still here to help her at times like this. Just like.....just like her dad. The dad who was hardly ever there, hardly ever had been. Even now when he lived ten minutes drive away she never saw him. His wife, her step mother, the bitch. Her fault. Shit, families hurt.

*****

133

Talk about deja vue. Nikki was back in her kitchen, the kids with their father, a bottle of wine on the table and her glass full to the brim and up to her lips. The only new thing from the old familiar scene was the nine inch Cook's knife beside the bottle. Since that night she had roamed the house armed to the teeth like some suburban soccer mom psycho pirate.

The tears welled up again, couldn't help it. She was remembering. She did a lot of remembering lately. She remembered standing at the door, seeing him climb off her son, the blood, the naked bodies. Heard the sobs, the snarl as Tim turned and came at her. She just held the scissors in front of her and he ran into them. Simple.

She heard his bellow of rage and pain again, too. He looked down and his eyes opened wide in anger. Not terror, he wasn't afraid of her or of dying or even of the fact he had just been stabbed. He was angry she had defied his authority and defiled his moment with her son, interrupting him in the middle of his due.

Nikki didn't step back, not with her son in front of her and that scum between them. She stepped forward and slapped his face. Hard! Again! Again! He stepped back with each slap and now she had enough room to step around him and put herself between him and her child. Hamish was now looking over his shoulder at his mum, now burying his head in the pillow in shame, sobbing through the gag chafing his mouth, feeling the pain and shame and blood from his arse trickle down his legs and pool near his crotch.

Tim didn't dare do anything. He realized by the third slap he had lost his control of Nikki. His power was no longer there. Even Hamish. He had had him and now he was just a piece of meat. Forget it. Not worth it. Not worth taking on this she animal in front of him. He felt the scissors in his stomach and knew he needed help quickly. He stepped back, away from the demon woman in front of him. He could see her anger, her disgust and her willingness to finish him off just in the set of her face. She was no longer pretty. She was savage. She wasn't even beautiful at the same time, just raw and angry and lethal. Dangerous.

With Hamish behind her, Nikki took a step forward. She had seen the change in Tim even as she slapped him the last time. He was beaten. Finished. No longer a threat. He was also bleeding. He still held on to the handle of the scissors, protruding from his stomach. How medieval.

"Get. Out. GET! OUT! GET OUT! GETTOUT! GETTTTTOWWWWT! Her order grew larger and more menacing each

134

time. Each time she took a step toward him. Each time he took a step backwards. As he stepped back out of the boy's bedroom, half falling against the door frame he turned and ran. He ran to her bedroom and snatched up his clothes. She stood in the hallway, halfway between the bedrooms of her two children and her own. On guard. Protecting. Doing what she should have done weeks ago and hating herself for not knowing. Not seeing what was in front of her very eyes. All that church going and the lies and she knew it was because she was greedy. Greedy for the affection of a good looking man nearly half her age. Ego. Greed. And her son had paid her dues with his innocence.

Tim had run out of the house and she hadn't heard of him since. No police came to the door and she never bothered to report to them. Why? Hamish had been through enough. What could dragging him through the court system achieve other than even more suffering? Tim was gone. If he came back she would kill him this time. She knew, she just knew she would and so did he. She had seen it in his face when he ran out the front door, looking wildly back over his shoulder at her, clutching his clothes in one hand and the handle of the scissors in the other.

She threw the rest of his clothes and few personal things into the skip and had watched them over the rim of her favourite coffee cup being driven away by the garbos. Then she called the kid's father, told him everything, he was over in a few hours. They agreed the kids needed a break from the house and she needed time to herself. No worries, call when you want them back, whatever Nikki, he had been great, amazing, as if the severity of the situation cancelled all the animosity of the past. Not for long of course but take it and appreciate it while you can.

She finished the glass of wine and poured another. She would pour another after that and when that bottle was empty, well she had stocked the cellar last week. She had at least three coma's worth of booze in the house. Why not? She only hung around for the kids and she hadn't been worth much for them lately. At least not poor Hamish. Poor, gentle Hamish. The crying started anew. She poured, drank, poured and drank again.

*****

"What do you mean she won't take custody of the baby?" Debbie asked her attorney again. "Jerry, she signed the contract, you said it was iron clad, no way out!" Debbie folded her arms across her chest and stared back at the lawyer. He moved uncomfortably in his chair for a few seconds, then settled and spoke.

"Debbie, you knew. You knew when you signed the contract that the baby was handicapped. You knew and you made no disclosure. She can rescind the contract in a heartbeat. And she has!" Jerry could have protected her against this if she had warned him. A simple clause, even a few words added, wouldn't have taken much. Before the contract was signed. Now, no way he could get her out of this.

"How can she prove I knew anything?" Debbie demanded.

"She can subpoena your pre-natal medical records, subpoena your doctor. She can do all of this and she will, believe me. Basically you entered into a legally binding contract withholding facts relevant to the contract. So relevant the contract would likely not have been signed if the other party had been aware of them. And you have a duty of disclosure, it's in the contract. You blew it Debbie. The baby is yours!"

Debbie rolled away from her visitor and faced the window. Again. Her standard position it seemed whenever she had visitors lately. She was going home tomorrow and it looked like she would have to take the baby with her. No! No way!

"Jerry. What if I wasn't fit to take care of the baby? What if I had the authorities test me and say I was unfit and the baby could not be under my care, what then?" Debbie was leading somewhere, Jerry could tell. He didn't like it but there was nothing about this entire business he liked. Hell! He wasn't being paid to like anything, he was paid to be her attorney.

"If you were unfit to take care of the child then he would be given to his.........father?" The last word came out like a question. Yes. Brilliant! Of course! He had been focusing so much on the contract, which only had to be between Debbie and Terri because......because John was a legal guardian or parent anyway. It was his child as much as it was Debbie's and that meant he has much right to access, but also the same responsibility to care for the baby.

"Debbie, you should have sat for the bar." Jerry beamed.

"Jerry, I sat at enough bars in my life to learn a few street tricks. Make me a bad mother. Go!" She was laughing now.

Jerry stuffed his papers into his briefcase and hit the door almost at a run, or as fast as was politically correct in a modern maternity ward.

Debbie rolled back and faced the window again, only this time she was smiling.

CHAPTER 17

"No Way! No Fucking, freaking way! No way are we taking that...that...that thing into our house!" Terri was really losing it John thought. Again. Only at least this time it was in the privacy of their own kitchen and not the maternity ward at the hospital. Like the last time. Not quite. This time she was angrier. If that were possible.

"John, we are not bringing up a spastic! No way! You tell her the contract is finished, over, not going to happen!" Terri was adamant. She knew enough to know there was no way Debbie could hold her to the contract. She had to have known the baby was not 100% when she signed the thing, non-disclosure like that was grounds for cancellation or rescission or whatever term they used. She knew that much for certain.

"Terri, I am the baby's father, there is nothing I can do. Debbie has been declared unfit to care for the child by DOCCS. If the Department of Child and Community Services says she can't have custody, that is water tight. They have a lot of power and there is nothing we can do. Honey, we have to take him." John was pleading with her and he hated himself for doing it. He knew she despised weakness in him but what could he do? He didn't want a retarded son in his life either, not enough in the sympathy vote to make the hassle worth while.

"Can't you hand him over to DOCCS, tell them you are unfit too?" Terri suggested.

"Sure, after we spent all that time and effort and not to mention money convincing them we were model parents and that they shouldn't argue against the arrangement with Debbie. Fat chance Terri." John started to regain some of his more in charge side as he accepted the reality, the finality, the legality of the situation. Debbie had him by the balls, he had been out maneuvered. OK. Time to regroup and think through his options, develop a new game plan. No point yelling at each other.

"Terri, we don't get the kid for another week, hospital won't let him go, still too premature or something. Debbie has been discharged and the hospital is looking after him. The social worker there suggested we both go and spend time with him, bond...you know?"

"Bond with him?" Terri turned to a bunch of celery sticks sitting on the bench top. She tossed the bunch at John, he scrambled to catch it instinctively and stop it hitting the floor. "Bond with that!" Terri turned and left the kitchen. John heard the bedroom door slam and the click of the lock as she shut him from her life for another night. He still held the celery. He put the vegetable down gently almost as if it were his son, then grabbed his keys and headed for the door, the bar, anywhere but here.

*****

"Alena, this is Chris. Chris, Alena". Pete stood back and took it in. The vibe. It looked positive, both people hadn't said anything yet, just kept staring into each other's eyes. Perfect. Pete had fancied his chances getting the two of them together would be a positive thing. Call it a gut instinct or whatever, but he had just known the two of them would hit it off.

Pete backed away as they started talking to each other, the small talk coming easily from both, always a good sign. Another good sign was the body language, open and inviting the other to get intimate. Then again both of them went at it like rabbits so they should be made for each other. He knew Alena did because he had been there with her. He knew Chris did because Chris told him often enough and he had met some of his girlfriends and even they said how much of a root rat he was.

Terrific, so now they have each other, which was fine with Pete. Things had gone sour for him with Alena the last two months or so. They hadn't done it for weeks and she knew he thought it was time they both moved on. They really liked each other as friends but the lust was over and done with and in some ways they were too alike to remain lovers. And sane, or whole, or not in trouble with the law for assault. Alena that is. She had a hell of a temper on her but Chris had the patience of a saint. Perfect match.

The backyard barby was going great, lots of good friends around and plenty of food and booze for all, music banging away on the stereo and what more could you ask for? Now if Pete could get laid tonight……..

It had been twenty minutes or so since he backed away from the pair and already they had disappeared. Probably off to her room for a quickie. Good for them, half their luck. Pete kept mingling with his guests and finally sat at a table with some old friends he hadn't seen since a long time when. The bourbon was doing its' job and the BBQ was finally glowing the way it should have done when he was trying to cook the meat. He was going to buy a gas BBQ next week for sure. Too much messing about with charcoal and who cared about a subtle nuance in taste? He couldn't make out the difference and gas was so much quicker and easier than huffing and puffing charcoal into shape.

He really needed to get out more. There were no new prospects for him here because these were all his mates and their wives or girlfriends. Nobody had brought a spare and so far the only bloke looking to get lucky tonight was already well away: Chris. Fine, time to work on Plan C. Get pissed. No point working Plan B, why pick a fight with your best friends? Especially at his age? Mind you, Pete had always chosen either Plan A or Plan C, never saw the point in starting a fight for the hell of it, what if you got the crap beaten out of you? How would that make your night more enjoyable? And if, like some, you picked on some poor sod who everybody knew couldn't punch their way out of a wet paper bag even if you left the thing open, where was the value in that? Plain bullying and thuggery, that. Never Pete's cup of tea.

*****

Terri felt a lot better. She had just spent hundreds of John's dollars on her hair and nails, more on new shoes, a dress and half a handbag full of new makeup, total expenditure over a thousand dollars. That would make any woman feel better, Terri certainly did and John should feel great. After all it was his suggestion she go and do a little shopping, buy something, make herself feel better. And she did feel better. Much better.

She parked her car in her space and checked herself once more in the mirror. Perfect. OK. Time to face the music and put her plan into operation. If she was going to have to play Mommy Dearest to some vegetable of a child she might as well look her best as often as she could, and John could afford it to be very often.

She hadn't been to the hospital to see the little wretch, no point. She had seen things like him before and she knew there was no way she would be bonding with it. Regardless of what the doctor and that full of herself bitch from the handicapped help group or whatever they called themselves said.

No doubt cerebral palsy is not the end of the world. Terri conceded the fact that inside was probably a child of above average intelligence who just had some difficulty communicating with the world and their own muscles and so on. Sure, no problem. But not her child.

Anyway, she would soon have the situation under control and everything would be wonderful. First things first, set her face so she didn't show the revulsion she felt and knew she would have trouble hiding when she would have to pick up the baby and cradle it in her arms. Luckily she could hide most of it's' weaknesses in the swaddling clothes. That was how she saw it really, weak. Not perfect. Not beautiful. Not worthy of her. She wondered not for the first time whether the weakness in the child was due to the mother or the father. Surely the mother, John couldn't have the gene that made that thing go off the rails, surely? Had to be her, at her age and everything. Shouldn't she have been menopausal or something? That would have done it. Bitch!

Terri climbed out of the car and locked it, then headed inside. Time to play dutiful mother of poor, handicapped step son. Give it a day or two, be seen here and there by the right people, evoke the right amount of sympathy, then deal with the matter. Once and for all. Perfect.

*****

Nikki hung up the phone. No way were they going to come around this time she thought. She had just rung the local church warden, his wife actually. Told her she was on her own again and not to send anyone around from that church of buggerers and nutcases, the last one was more than enough, thank you. Of course the poor woman had been beside herself and obviously distressed to hear the details. Not too distressed though. Still able to start hinting perhaps Nikki was to blame, not enough faith and all that rubbish. Nikki had heard enough and simply hung up the phone.

She wondered when or even if, her children would ever feel safe coming back here. She hadn't seen them for two weeks now, or was it three? She had lost all track of time. Luckily her boss had understood and let her take the time she needed. Of course she knew they couldn't keep paying her salary and not getting any work from her. She would call her boss and see if they had something for her to do. Something simple and absorbing but not too taxing.

The glass of wine raised itself to her lips without her having to ask and she took a sip, then let the glass return to the table. Starting to have a mind of its own, that glass. Knew when to refill itself and that seemed like quite often. Nikki was losing track of how much she was drinking, when she was drinking and if it wasn't for the empties waiting by the garbage bin for an audit she would be worried about it.

She had a permanent buzz on now. Lived drunk. Well, not exactly drunk but definitely not sober. No way she could face the day sober so she had to be somewhere in between. It wasn't tipsy, that was a happy semi-drunk state. She was past that, actually she had never made it to tipsy. Went from stone cold sober and depressed to roaring drunk and depressed to blind drunk and depressed to now constantly drunk and depressed. She wasn't sure which was the common denominator, the depression or the drunkenness? Did it matter? Yes it did. She didn't mind being a drunkard, even an alcoholic if that were her fate. But a manic depressive? Mentally ill? Her? Never!

For all her avant garde new agey ways, Nikki still had an old fashioned industrial age view of mental illness. To her, as to many, it was a weakness as well as a sickness. It was something more, something more insipid, more insidious, more shameful. Shame. Yes. That was the word. Shame. Shameful. Something to be ashamed of. Not like having breast cancer or Crohn's Disease. No. Depression was a mental illness and that made you a mental patient and so therefore a looney, a nutcase, a wacko.

She could not see any correlation between an ailment afflicting an organ such as the stomach and a mental condition. One made you shit for weeks and the other made you a shit for life. No! Depression and paranoia and schizophrenia and all those other phobia ridden conditions happened to weird people. Sick, twisted people who killed everyone with axes and chainsaws and then raped small boys and ran around naked and drooling with their hair all messed up and not having seen a comb in a month of Sundays. That was mental illness. Depression.

No. Far better she accept the fact she was a drunk. A lush. A boozer. An alcoholic. She had once called her father an alcoholic and he had vehemently denied her allegation. "Nikki dear there is no way I am an alcoholic. A drunkard yes, but an alcoholic? Be honest sweetie. Can you see me making it to all those meetings?"

She laughed again as she remembered her father saying that. He had died a week later. Run over by a bus. On his way to an AA meeting. Which was the exact moment she imploded and tears told their story on her cheeks for the third time in as many hours. Uncontrollable sobbing, no idea where it welled up from, it just happened. She let it happen. It was good for the soul apparently. Unless it was a symptom of an undiagnosed mental condition. Shit!

*****

Pete was going to call the council pound. Alena and Chris were still joined at the lip like a couple of rutting mongrel dogs. They hadn't let go of each other for hours, not since they crawled out of her room into the wan light of day as Pete's vacuuming woke them from their slumber. That and the fact they both had mouths dryer than an Arab's sock from all the talking, kissing, alcohol drinking and whatever else sucked the moisture out of you.

He watched them pashing off on his sofa and decided he had seen enough of this. Since Alena lived here too and her rent was paid up he could hardly kick them out. He got up and grabbed his keys and wallet, then headed for the door. They didn't even look up as he bade them a good bye and headed for his truck.

Pete was hungry and figured a quick trip to the local strip mall and some greasy fast food should sort him out. Maybe drop by the bottle shop and get some booze to replace the hit his bar had taken last night. Maybe just drive around for a while first. Maybe hit the highway and see if any working girls were on duty near the petrol station. Pete didn't mind a cheap blowjob in the car, got the job done. Not great sex although he had known a few true professionals who even for fifty bucks gave excellent head.

He started to think about what made great sex great as he drove around. Sex itself, intercourse or penetration or whatever was the latest buzzword, what made that any better with one woman than another? He had slipped it to sleeping beauties and it was still alright, they did nothing, just lay there comatose and oblivious. Other girls thrashed like wild things but did their enthusiasm and energy make it any better "sex"?

Oral sex was different. That was a variation where talent and skill and technique really played a part, giving or getting. Some women were just naturals at it and seemed to know exactly how to make a man suck the mattress up his butt they were that good. Others just wailed away until the pain was too much to stand and the "victim" stopped her and jacked himself off to finish.

Then there were the girls without a clue. Totally bereft of any idea of what they were supposed to be doing. Probably hated the whole idea of giving head. And then there were those great givers once again. Oh yeah, you didn't come across them too often but when you did, you never wanted to let them go. Alena was not the best at head. Great fuck and thrash galore but blow jobs were not her thing.

Terri was good at both but particularly exceptional at blowjobs. Pete missed her blowjobs. Pete missed her pussy for penetration and he missed her as his wife and friend. His arousal started to ebb as his thoughts moved on from what made some women hot in the cot and others not. Hah! He was a poet and he don't know it. Didn't help. Thoughts of Terri came flooding back. Filling his mind with memories, snatches of conversations, vignettes of special moments.

He remembered their first night together. First date actually. They couldn't get enough of each other and stayed out so late it was almost dawn when they fell into bed. He promised not to take advantage of her, swore he wasn't just going to screw her and then never call. He meant it. She was the hottest, prettiest woman he had ever been with, no way was he letting her go. And he didn't, did he? Married her a year later. Proposed to her after a month and then he had forced himself to wait another two weeks from when he knew he would ask until popping the question. She had known by then. Knew all along. Knew he would propose. Knew she would say yes. They both knew.

That first night. That first time. She had cried. They came together. And she cried. Great sex? No, more than that. Much, much more. Real love. Two people being as close as they could be. In tune, as one, just like they say on the romance web sites. Soul mates. Only now she had taken her soul and mated with someone else. Shit!

*****

Debbie was crying again. She missed her son, her only remaining memento of all her years with John. She didn't count the furniture, artifacts clothes and jewelry. She didn't count her own two girls as they had already been on the scene when she met John. She only counted her son. Her spastic son. Or was he autistic? Or just handicapped? Or just challenged or special or whatever the hell they called it nowadays?

He was all she had and she had let him go. She knew she couldn't raise him but that wasn't why she let him go. That wasn't the reason she had her lawyer make sure her doctor declared her unfit to be a mother. Dodgy, sure, but totally unfit? Of course not. She would have managed somehow, of course she would have. She knew that all along. She knew John would give her enough money to bring up the kid, hire a nurse or nanny and still live well. She knew all that. She also knew why she had given her son away.

Her. Floppsy moppsy. The bitch. The whore. The slag, the slut, the cow, the list of names and invective that did no good no matter how much she spewed out her hatred in definite articles and nouns. Even throwing in adjectives made no difference. The fat mole. She wasn't fat.

The ugly whore, damn she was stunning. Adjectives made it worse. She had nothing over her, that's why it hurt, that's why men went for younger, prettier mistresses. To punish their older, uglier, time worn wives.

And she had nothing. Nothing. The only thing she had she had signed away. Just to spite her rival, the woman who had stolen her man. Or maybe won him in a fair fight. A fight all women had been competing in since time began. There was plenty of sperm out there, it was her eggs that had value. Her eggs that needed the best, the biggest, the strongest male to fertilize them. John was her alpha male and he had been lured away by a younger female. A tale as old as mankind.

So what? She still had nothing. Nothing left. Nothing to cling to for hope. Alone. Her kids were grown and gone, couldn't wait to get out. She had had a chance to start again, maybe stay close to John through their son and she lost that. Lost? Threw it away because their son was not perfect. He was corrupted and she knew that would hurt that bitch more than anything else. Not the pretty little boy she had wanted to parade in front of all their friends. Her old friends a lot of them. Funny how they are her friends now. And his still. But not Debbie's. No. Not now she isn't John and Debbie. Or Debbie and John. Not now she is just Debbie, John's ex-wife. The older one. The much older one.

She filled her glass again and drank the contents in two swallows. What now? What did she do now? Where did she turn? Who did she look to for friendship? Solace? Advice? She thought of Pete, the bitches' husband. He had made it clear though he didn't want to waste time and emotion crying on each other's shoulders. Almost as if blamed her for not keeping her man on a leash. Well what about him and his slut? Maybe if he had kept her in the manner to which she was quickly becoming accustomed she wouldn't have gone after her John.

She was running out of friends. New people she met quickly tired of her ad nauseum regurgitation of the tawdry details of the divorce. She had shaved her divorce story down to the Reader's Digest version too, much like most people in the same boat she had met had done. At first you tell it all, every nuance, every event. Then you start to gloss over some details, leave other things out, cut it down to the nuts and bolts and bring it as close to today as you can and make sure you show how it no longer bothers you. Yeah right.

She had nothing now, not even the energy or the audience to rehash the full details. The pregnancy and birth and subsequent condition and handing over of the baby had added a little spice to the tale but that soon paled. Now she knew if she tried to explain why she didn't have the baby she only made herself look either incompetent or nasty. She didn't think of herself as either and didn't want others to have to make a choice. It was getting simpler to simply say nothing.

So now she couldn't even talk to people about it. Nothing, absolutely nothing left in her life. Why bother? Why go on? Why keep living? Who would want her? Almost half a century of wear and tear and two walk in closets full of emotional baggage and tiresome skeletons. No way she would ever love again, so why live? Why?

CHAPTER 18

"I'm sorry. Your...baby. Your baby didn't make it, I'm really terribly sorry..." The doctor looked away. He couldn't bring himself to look into the teary red orbs this otherwise beautiful young woman had for eyes and tell her anything more than the shallow explanation he had just given her. Didn't make it. Didn't make what? The grade? The first half of his life? Hell the poor thing wasn't a month old and even though his life expectancy was naturally going to be shorter than a normal child's it would have been a damn site longer than a fortnight.

Make it? Didn't make it? Terri thought the little prick was never going to friggin' die for christ's sake. She had cradled his twisted form so his face was in the cleft of her armpit, just like she had practiced with her life size and lifelike Jeremimah doll. Pete had bought her that doll. Cost him eight hundred dollars but it was the start of her collection and it was so perfect. So lifelike and real. A beautiful black baby girl that nearly everybody who saw it thought it was a real live baby.

More real and far more perfect than that twisted wretch of a spastic mutant. Terri screwed up her face unconsciously as she despised the poor thing once more for taking so long to suffocate. She'd killed it in plain sight of doctors and nurses and nobody had been the wiser. Just loosened the wrap and eased the kid around in the swaddling until his face was in the cleft of her armpit. Nice, tight squeeze and croon a soft lullaby while gently rocking the mongrel to sleep. A long, deep, lasting sleep. Then put him down and rearrange the wrap and he really looked so peaceful as if he was sleeping, his little Mongol face barely peeking out of the wrap so a casual glance by a passing nurse wouldn't notice his rapidly changing colour.

Didn't make it? He was never going to make it doctor. Terri sat down and sobbed with relief it was all over and she was starting to get the sympathy that was her due. Truly, nobody was the wiser and it would take very sophisticated forensic examination to detect any foul play. And who would even consider asking the questions that might lead to the right answers? Terri was, after all, the dutiful wife of the estranged father, stepping in and nobly taking on a handicapped child as a demonstration of her love for her new man. That was the way Terri had sorted it all out in her mind and that was the way it was all coming together. Murder truly is easy to get away with if nobody suspects you and even easier if there is no suspicion of murder in the first place.

Terri made a visible effort at pulling herself together, although not too completely. The baby had been taken away, she had declined the offer of a final viewing and a chance to say goodbye. "I hardly had time to say hello…no, let my last memories of him be of him alive…" That had almost brought the house down in tears despite the staff having seen more tragedy than any of them had ever thought they could in an eight hour shift and still turn up for work every day.

"I want to be with his father now, please, someone call me a taxi…" and several interns and half a dozen wardsmen had rushed off to play the Gallant Knight and arrange her carriage home. As she left the hospital grounds she barely looked back over her shoulder out the back window of the cab. Those staff still watching half raised hands to wave goodbye but instinctively thought better of it under the circumstances and made various vague grooming actions with the offending hands instead.

They noticed she had a half smile on her face as she turned back away from their direction. Perhaps she was thinking of a smile or a thumb squeeze the baby had given her while she cradled him. Perhaps it was a twisted grimace of sadness at her loss?

As she turned back to look out the windscreen of the cab, past the driver's left ear and over the top of the ticking meter Terri smiled. She had done it. She now had all the benefits of being the bereaved new mother without the crap her life would have been had she had to raise the monster. Excellent. Now it was time to work the grief for all it was worth and get John to take her overseas. Paris maybe? Or Los Angeles? Yes. L.A. John had been murmuring about chasing a promotion in the L.A. office, time she pushed him into getting the damn thing. House in Beverley Hills or Malibu might be just the ticket. Leave the details of the divorce to her lawyer and get away. Start afresh. Start new. Clean slate. Her and John. Make a baby of their own but check it before it hatches to make sure there isn't a repeat of the last fiasco. Damn that bugger of a thing took forever to go.

*****

"You can stand either there or here Mr. Graham, it doesn't matter." The Judge explained.

"Thank You Your Worship but I stood on the right when I married her and I stand in the right today, so I'll stand here to the right if it pleases the court." was Pete's reply. It received a ripple of appreciation from the gallery and a smile from the Judge. This was the fifteenth matter she had heard this morning and she had another twenty five divorces to go through before her day would be done. No wonder the process was compared to some kind of sausage machine.

Estranged, irreconcilably and irretrievably broken down couples came in the main door, took a seat until it was their turn then stood in front of the Judge. She asked them if the marriage was doomed, were there any children, what steps had been taken to handle custody and support if there were and providing all the tees had been crossed and the eyes dotted, she declared the marriage a draw and have a decree nisi for lunch, your decree absolute will be posted to you in a month.

The couple before Pete had been together twenty four years and simply grown apart. The kids were grown and gone and going through their own marital traumas and so there was no reason the Judge could see to prolong either party's agony. Go away, you are no longer man and wife.

The solicitor for his wife stood obligingly to one side and then took up his place on the left. The Judge read through the petition, assured herself there were no children of the marriage to worry about and that the marriage had irretrievably broken down and so declared decree nisi at thirty five minutes past ten of the clock in the morning, decree absolute will be declared a month from today now bugger off. Lapsed time….1 minute 58 seconds.

Pete didn't even notice the solicitor trying to make amends for his squeezing the last penny from Pete during the property settlement phase, Pete no longer cared anyway. She had her share, he had what was left. It was over. She wasn't even in the country anymore according to what the solicitor had told the judge. He was a free man, not that he had ever felt imprisoned by his marriage. He had entered into the arrangement of his own free will, in fact let's not forget it was he who had proposed to her.

Funny how that works. The man is led to think he is the one who chooses the wife but the reality is the opposite. She chooses him. All along the man has to prove he is the one for her and she gets the easy job of saying yes or no. He asks her for a dance and she decides if they dance together. He asks if he can buy her a drink, take her to the movies, out for dinner whatever. He asks and she is the one to say yes or no. So who is running the show? Who is truly in charge?

If she is ugly she might find it slow going waiting for dates and dances but eventually even the least physically appealing of the female

148

species seems to get her man. The woman is screening the man of course. A feint heart never won a fair maiden so if he lacks the guts to ask her out he misses out, simple as that. Women truly aren't as big on looks as men are. It is important to them, no matter what they may say to the contrary but not as important as it is to a man. After all, the man needs the physical attraction so he can get it up and perform. She needs a provider, someone who can give her what she needs and take care of her while she is vulnerable to the ravages of nature while breeding and weaning her offspring.

And that is pretty much why Pete was walking out of the Family Court building a divorced man. Not single. He would never be single again. Divorced. Forever divorced. Forever tainted in a way, second hand goods. Some other woman's cast off. In future, forms he would have to fill out would include the query on his civil status and he would have to tick "divorced". Not single, never married, widowed or married. Divorced. Failed. Blew it. Loser.

Pete looked up and down the wind swept city street and wondered what to do next. He had taken the day off work to attend the hearing, even though he didn't have to. But he did have to. He had to see it through to the end. The bitter end. He had been there at the start and he was damn well going to be there at the end. And he had been and it was the end now. Ended. Over with. Finished. Done.

He crossed the street when common sense and a break in the traffic dictated rather than wait until some green man started to flash his permission to cross. He walked past a Malaysian restaurant that was already open for an early lunch and so, at a few minutes after eleven, he went in and sat down. By himself. A free man. Almost hungry. Christ he missed his wife.

*****

John knew, he just knew. Terri had….Terri had…. He couldn't bring his mind to state it openly but he knew what he was avoiding admitting. Still, problem solved really. He had no feelings towards the child either way, he might have had if it hadn't been… Hadn't been, well…..wrong. He looked across at Terri, sleeping in the giant hotel bed in their suite in the Wiltshire Hotel, then looked back out the window over Wiltshire Boulevard towards Rodeo Drive. Terri's POW's from her raid on Rodeo were still lined up awaiting execution over by the walk in robe. She had taken half the drive prisoner by the look of all those designer label bags.

Armani, Gucci, Chanel, Klein, Hilfiger and half a dozen more. Must have cost him a fortune but worth every dime. The sex tonight had been better than even their first night together.

His attorney had left a message with the desk telling him her divorce had been approved and she was now free. Free to marry John. If she wanted to. And why wouldn't she? John's insecurities came flooding back and washed over him like a tsunami. For a corporate mover and shaker in a million dollar a year job, plus stock options and bonuses, he had moments of doubt in his personal life that never entered his working world.

John was as cut throat in the board room as any of his company, a firm known worldwide for being ruthless and mean, not to mention downright nasty when they chose. If some of the other corporate giants and captains of industry he had made feel small knew how fragile his ego was when it came to his personal life, they would have taken heart and worked that knowledge to their advantage.

If they had known he had found his new trophy wife in a brothel they would have gone to town, or at least had the confidence to stand firm if not the bad manners to mention their knowledge. John hid his personal failings well and like many so called successful men, he knew he teetered on a knife edge. He was up so high if he fell he would fall farther than most could safely climb back from. Some men had made and lost more than one fortune in their lives but John was not that kind of man. If he lost the fortune he was making now there would be no coming back and he knew it. He also knew part of his wealth was his wife. Or hopefully soon to be wife. No time to waste. Get his divorce through as quick as he could arrange it and get Terri signed up. Close the deal. If he could he'd get his people on it first thing, just that he couldn't do that with Terri. He was it. It was up to him. He'd call reception and have them organize some flowers. Play the romantic suitor, that was the plan.

John turned away from the window and climbed back into the big bed, snuggled up to Terri and closed his eyes. He felt her stir as he eased closer to her back and spooned her with his own body. His Terri, his wife. Soon, very soon.

*****

Chris rolled off Alena and lay flat on his back, spread eagled and staring at the ceiling. He was spent. Exhausted. Finished. Drained. She had cleaned him out and he was…..satiated. At last he got to use the word he lost the spelling competition over way back in high school. He had never felt satiated before, probably why he had never been able to spell the damn word. He was satiated now.

Alena closed her eyes and then opened them again, almost as if she were checking if they still worked. She had screwed them shut so tightly while the orgasm washed over her she felt she may have to recalibrate her eyeballs or something. She was as relaxed as she had ever been in her life. She was in love and she knew Chris loved her too. She knew, she just knew.

She also knew she was pregnant. She didn't know how she knew, she just knew. She was pretty sure when, too. The doorway bang. Not that it could be proven or even mattered. They had done it so many times in the past few months there seemed to be no letting up. She was a nymphomaniac, she was sure of that. Although maybe not. Not now she had Chris. She had read in some woman's magazine that true nympho's can't orgasm. That's why they keep wanting more and more sex. Yet she could come, she just couldn't come enough to satisfy her craving for more orgasms.

Chris had always been highly sexed, too sexed for his first wife's tastes. Cold cow. She had hardly put out when they were courting and once they were married it had dried up to once a week if he begged. After the kids came on the scene he was lucky if he got it once a month. Then the bitch came clean she had been screwing that Maori prick for months.

So now he was living in a caravan park shagging his brains out with an eighteen year old nymphet and having the time of his life. And he loved her. It hit him like a bolt from the blue. He did love her, he really did love her. He was sixteen years her senior as they say in the tabloids but he really didn't care. She had two kids she had given up for adoption and he had two kids his bitch ex wife would never let him see again the way things were going but at least he had Alena and she had him. Maybe one day they would start a family all their own. Maybe.

Alena looked at Chris at the precise moment he looked at her. Both of them felt it and they instinctively fell back into each other's arms. What was it about the other one, each thought? How come we are so right for each other? Why couldn't I have met him five years ago? Why couldn't I have met her ten years ago? Why did life do what it did to us and play this painful numbers game neither of us agreed to the rules of or have any say in? Who cares how many years are between us, we didn't pick when we wanted to be born.

They made love again. Less hurried but no less urgently than every time before this one. More tender each time but harsh enough nevertheless as they drained the other yet willingly gave themselves for the taking. If two people were meant to be, they were them.

"Chris?"

"Alena?"

"I'm pregnant."

"I know."

"You know? How?"

"Dunno how. I just know. How do you know?"

"Dunno how. I just know."

"I love you.'

"I know. Love you too."

*****

Debbie rolled onto her side and looked at the clock on the bedside table only there wasn't a clock there. She rolled over onto her other side and looked at the other bedside table and there wasn't even a bedside table. She felt a momentary stab of panic then relaxed. Why worry? At the same moment she gave up worrying about missing clocks and non existent bedroom furniture she remembered she wasn't in her home anymore.

She didn't have a home. His lawyer had seen to that. Better lawyer than hers. More expensive. Did he charge more because he was better or was he better because he charged more? Or did part of his four hundred dollars an hour fee go to the judge to make sure he did better than her lawyer at a hundred and fifty dollars an hour? Who cares? It was over and done with anyway so why worry?

Trying to get a fair share of their property when she was going against the best hired gun in the corporate world with a suburban ambulance chaser was akin to trying to get an Indonesian court to believe blowing people up was worse than getting them high some other way. But why worry?

She rolled back and lay staring at the ceiling, wondering absent mindedly about the weird stain around the cheapest, nastiest light fitting she had ever seen in any room in her life. No way would she have that in her house, but then she didn't have a house any more, did she? He had sold it up on her while she was still in rehab and then took the money with him to the States. Probably bought his floozy a ring or something with it.

She didn't have a car either but that was her fault. Well his really but she had been driving it at the time. She had been drinking before she was driving but he had driven her to the drink. Him. Her. And that high priced lawyer. They probably had someone drive them to the drink and then back again. They had homes to go to. At nearly half a grand an hour the bastard attorney could probably hire someone to do his drinking for him as well as his driving. Prick.

But why worry? Screw them. Screw him. Screw her. Screw the lot of them. Christ how friggin long did these pills take to work? Shit she needed to pee. Screw it. Pee here. Who cares? Why fuckin' worry? She didn't have to clean the damn bed. Damn you John. I miss you. Jesus that piss is warm.

*****

Nikki noticed the good looking bloke sitting by himself with a nasi goreng and a beer. A bit younger than her, late thirties maybe but older than Tim. No way she'd have another Tim in her life. This bloke looked, well, he just looked different. Nice. Warm. Loving. Soft yet hard. Tough but understanding…. Oh for heaven's sake get a grip woman you've been reading too many Mills and Boones she laughed to herself.

Pete looked up and saw her staring at him. She was staring. Looking intently, longer than socially accepted for a casual yet inquisitive glance or whatever the duration was supposed to be. Nice. Good looking woman. Older than him maybe, maybe not. She looked good. If she was older than thirty five then she kept herself in shape. Nice dark hair, great body.

He's seen me staring. Shit. Stop being stupid. You're like a bloody schoolgirl. Get a grip!

Why not? Just go over there and ask her to join you for lunch. No harm and the worse she could say is bugger off and make you look like a drongo in a crowded restaurant. The restaurant was crowded now, the lunch time crowd had filtered in behind his notice while he had flicked through some old Asian Business Reviews.

He's coming over. I'm a mess. My hair. Damn.

"Hi. I couldn't help but notice you were staring at me." He had a nice, deep tenor like voice.

"St st st st st, staring? I guess I was, er, umm, ssssorry I er, well…"

She was articulate, kind of. Sounded educated anyway so no bimbo.

"Would you care to join me at my table, I have a much better view there."

"View? Of what? We're indoors, not a window in the place…?"

"Of me. Better view of me. You won't have to stare so hard and…..neither will I. My name's Pete, Pete Graham. I'm divorced."

Nikki laughed and took the proffered hand and shook it, firmly and without breaking eye contact. "Thank you Pete, Pete Graham. Divorced. My name is Nikki, Nikki Taylor. I'm not sure what I am to be honest."

*****

Pete rolled onto his side and looked at the still warm depression in the mattress that had until only moments before been the sleeping form of Nikki. She had lain in his bed, half covered with a sheet and spilling her hair over the pillow like a clichéd shampoo commercial. She was the one. He knew, he just knew. She was the one for him.

He swung his legs over the edge of the bed and stood up, grabbed his shorts from the dresser where they had landed after being flung with what could genuinely be called mad abandon and slipped them on. She was the one. He knew it. She knew it. But she wouldn't let herself be hurt ever again. So she was going. Now. Thanks, it had been the best ever but she couldn't risk it becoming like all the others had.

Pete had said nothing. What was there to say? What could he have said when she had made her mind up before she ever met him or anyone else and she wasn't going to be swayed. Why even try? What might they have shared if she hadn't shared so much pain and suffering before she met him. Why meet her now and not before? Why not meet her ten years from now and all would be ok by then. Or would it be? Would she ever be able to give herself to a man again? No matter how nice, how right, how perfect?

Would anything he could have said to a woman he had known for a month yet had searched for all his life time made her stay? Made her change her mind? If she had made up that mind that he found so alluring and attractive and yet would compromise herself for him after a few glib words would she still be the woman he wanted more than any other?

Was she the one and would he live forever after wondering? Was she just a ship passing in the night or his true soulmate? He would never know now and neither would she, if she ever bothered to dwell and ask the same question some time from now. How long before she kicked herself for losing him? Or found another Pete. If he were one in a million, as her favourite song said, there were another 4 just like him in New South Wales alone.

Pete climbed back into bed, unable to sleep because of his emotions. The heat. His gut. Nikki was....had been....something special. Something rare and beautiful. Something so neat. She was what every man really wanted...a good woman. He turned his pillow over and settled down into the relief it offered. That was it. All his life had been just like that. Feels great at first but you know it won't last. Just like the cool side of the pillow.